THE LAST R

THE MONSTER had a hundred hands—hands as delicate as the teazles that are still used in cloth factories. But more important it had a brain constructed of very fine wire and enlivened by little electric currents, like those which cause thought in the human brain and which stimulate nerves and move muscles. It could think logically and clearly—it beat its inventor at chess—and it could work tirelessly and move rapidly on its four iron legs.

Such was the machine invented by Ablard Pender—a thinking beast of steel and wire far stronger than a man or any animal. Down at the factory in the lonely Essex marshes Pender fondly imagined the beasts were under his control, but with its superior brain it quickly learned to reproduce itself and multiply at an alarming rate. Mysterious things began to happen—in the immediate neighbourhood—watches lost time, trains were delayed or stopped altogether, buses and cars refused to go. The machines had at last run amok and civilization was threatened by the last and most deadly revolution of all.

The excitement and tension of this story mounts with every chapter until the frankenstein revolution is finally conquered. In austere, almost biblical language Lord Dunsany has achieved a novel that no one else save Wells could have written.

THE LAST REVOLUTION

A Novel

Lord Dunsany

TALOS PRESS

First published by Jarrolds Publishers, 1951

First Talos Press edition 2015

Talos Press books may be purchased in bulk at special discounts for sales promotion, corporate gifts, fund-raising, or educational purposes. Special editions can also be created to specifications. For details, contact the Special Sales Department, Talos Press, 307 West 36th Street, 11th Floor, New York, NY 10018 or info@skyhorsepublishing.com.

Talos Press is an imprint of Skyhorse Publishing, Inc.®, a Delaware corporation.

Visit our website at www.skyhorsepublishing.com.

10 9 8 7 6 5 4 3 2 1

Library of Congress Cataloging-in-Publication Data is available on file.

Cover design by David Sankey
Cover photo courtesy of the estate of Lord Dunsany

Print ISBN: 978-1-940456-12-6
Ebook ISBN 978-1-940456-17-1

Printed in the United States of America

CHAPTER I

THE United Schools Club, or the Schools United as it is sometimes called, has so large a membership that the subscriptions, though low, are able to provide a club-house in the West End that has a good many comforts to atone for a certain crowding. I can get a hair-cut and a shampoo, for instance, there, the use of a typewriter even, or a secretary if I want one, and there is quite a good wine-cellar. Members are supposed to have been at some public school, but in practice that is not insisted on. I was sitting there one day in the reading-room near to a man that I did not know, who turned out to be Ablard Pender, about whom this story is told, and more than one or two members as they passed him in his chair where he was reading a newspaper said: "Hullo, Pender, I hear you have made a Frankenstein." Or, "Hullo, Pender. They tell me you've made a Frankenstein." The remark didn't vary very much. Nor does one expect a continual flow of originality in the reading-room of a club. It is enough if one has a few papers to read, and a comfortable chair in which to read them, and perhaps an occasional greeting from people one knows, without any profundity in it. So now people were saying, as they passed Ablard Pender's chair: "Good morning, Pender. I hear you have made a Frankenstein." I hadn't noticed Pender's answers at first; and then I heard him say: "Oh no, I haven't. But I have made a brain."

And the other member passed on like the rest, as he wanted to get a paper, and was evidently not particularly interested in Pender. Nobody was very much interested in Pender at the United. For one thing he did no work, or what they called work, so that he had no part in the life that any of them were leading. He lived on the proceeds of inventions that he had made, things so absurdly trivial that it is humiliat-

5

ing to think that only one member of the human race had been able to think of them. There is for instance no way of opening the ordinary envelope, if it is properly stuck. One has to detach a corner with a finger-nail, and then tear as well as one can. Pender invented an envelope that would open at once, and calculated that he saved millions of minutes in London alone; I think he said in a day, but it may have been in a year. Anyway he made money by it, and nobody else had seemed able to think of it. And then he was one of the men, but they have been very few, who invented the way of putting the shade of electric lights between the eye and the bulb, instead of on the far side of it. That brings him in some money too, though this invention is not much in use yet. And then he had a wonderful invention for concealing the pipes of plumbers. This didn't catch on very much, for plumbers are proud of their pipes and naturally like to show them, but it brought him in some money too. What really kept him going was a certain knack he had of seeing the perfectly obvious; simple things overlooked by everyone else, and an absolute confidence that he would always be able to see such simple things, and so make a steady income every year without ever having to save. He had a house at Kingston Hill with a little garden in front with a rhododendron in it, and a kitchen-garden behind; and a garage and a car. And he came up to the United whenever he liked, and sat there and read the papers and went home when he liked. He had not many friends, because he shared the work of none of them, and because they were unable to see the simple things he could see. But a few of them were greeting him now, and Pender was saying: "No, only a brain." Well, no one was much interested, because they had only inquired about his invention because they felt they must say something as they went by, and they went on to their papers or to look at the news on the tape. But I was interested and I said to him: "If you don't mind my butting in, you say you have made a brain?"

"Yes," he said. "I have made one out of fine wire."

"Out of wire?" I asked.

"Yes," he said, "quantities of wire, and little electric currents like what cause thought in our own brains and which stimulate nerves which move muscles."

"What is it like?" I asked.

"Just a round mass of minute wires," he said, "rather larger than our brains."

"But can it think?" I asked.

"Quite as well as ours," said Pender.

"That is very interesting," I said.

"It is in a way," he answered, and I didn't get any more information from him about the new brain at that time. After all, a club is not a scientific assembly, and one has papers to read there and one thing and another and one doesn't thrash anything out to its logical final conclusion. But one or two more members spoke to Pender and later on I joined in again, and what we got out of him was that at present the brain could only think, which it did very well, but that later on he was going to give it some sort of a body. It had ears already.

"Ears?" I said in some surprise.

"Oh that was very simple," said Pender. "An ear-drum is easily made. Why, even a common gong will hear you if you shout at it quite close; and you can actually hear it receiving the vibrations. And my wires convey the sounds farther in, to the brain. No, there was no difficulty in that. And I often talk to it. I have taught it chess already. The only difficulty is at present that it has so few ways of expressing itself. But I shall give it that."

"Will you really?" I said, or something of that sort.

"I am thinking of giving it a hundred hands," he said. "They are quite easily made. Claw-like things as delicate as a teazle. You know they use teazles still in the cloth factories——"

"A hundred hands?" I said.

"Yes," said Pender. "And look at all the work he will do for us. Twenty-four hours a day. No pay. No food, unless

you count a little oil. And never a holiday; always at work.
It will give us the leisure that slaves used to give the Romans."

"And what about legs?" I said, as I felt it was my turn
to say something.

"I shall give it enough to get about with," he said. "I was
thinking of four."

And then another member came up. "Talking about your
Frankenstein?" he said.

"My brain," said Pender.

"But you're going to give it a body, aren't you?" the
other said.

"Yes, in time," said Pender.

How trivial it all seems now, that talk in the club, compared with the astounding things that occurred when
Pender's invention got into its crab-like stride.

"And what about the trades unions?" said the other
fellow, a man called Weathery.

"The trades unions?" said Pender. "Why?"

"Won't they object?" asked Weathery.

"No," said Pender. "How can they? They don't object
if I keep a simple machine for stamping my own note-
paper. I can turn out what I like with my own machine."

"And what will you turn out?" asked Weathery.

"More machines," said Pender. "It is what the country
wants. The more work is done by machines, the more leisure
there is for men."

It is curious to think how out of date a man may be made
by merely an active brain. It often gets him engrossed with
something, while other people are drifting along together;
so that quite common minds may be in touch with what is
going on, while he may be thinking things like this, that
were being thought by everyone in the last century.

For several weeks I saw no more of Ablard Pender.
Sometimes I went again to the United, but Pender was not
there, and though his story lurked in my mind I forgot him.
What I could not forget, however, was that a new power had
been added to machines, which had seemed to me for some

time to be powerful enough already, an additional touch that appeared to me to give them the only thing that they lacked. They were far stronger than men as it was, or than any animal. Who would not rather be charged by an elephant than by a railway train, by a lion than by a fast car? Once I heard Pender's name mentioned in the club, but still I did not see him, or hear much news of him either. "What's Pender doing?" said somebody. "Playing about with wires and hooks and what he calls crank-shafts, I believe," said somebody else. That is all we heard of Pender. And then one day in that same reading-room of the club I saw him. I remembered at once all he had told us; seeing him there brought it back to me, and I was about to ask him after his metal brain, when he blurted out to me: "I have given it hands. It is actually working. I have only to give it legs and it will be a complete body."

"How many hands?" I asked.

"A hundred," he said, just as he had told us.

Others came up and he told them about his new invention too. What I chiefly remember is that he had been playing chess with it. I don't know that all of them believed him, but most of them did, for they knew at the Schools United that he had a knack of inventing things, and the necessary industry, which not every man has, to perfect them. And one or two more in neighbouring chairs turned and listened, as men will in clubs, when they hear anyone raising his voice.

"And can it really think?" asked one of them.

"It can beat me at chess," said Pender.

"Really?" said the man. "That's clever of it. But perhaps chess is not such a difficult game, if you don't play it the way the professionals do."

Whoever he was, he evidently did not play chess, or he would have known that Pender was one of the best players in the club; and the United had played chess matches against most of the chess-playing clubs, always with Pender on their team, and the club was much feared as an opponent. This made me think. If that machine could beat Pender at chess, here was something able to challenge the human intellect, if it got loose.

"You keep it under lock and key of course," I said anxiously to Pender.

"Oh, that's not necessary," said Pender. "It does whatever I tell it."

And then the evening papers came into the club, and I started reading one of them, and so did Pender, and I heard no more that day about his strange machine. Nor did I see Pender again at the club for several weeks. And during that time we heard that he had made another of his simple inventions that nobody else could think of. There aren't so many servants now as there used to be, but all that there are, when they hand you a dish, slant it so that the gravy is nearest to you. If it be a rectangular dish with corners that we will name after the compass, north-west, north-east, south-east and south-west and you are to the east of it, all waiters, except those that dump the contents into your plate with their own hands, will lean the dish towards you so that the gravy runs to south-east. You then have to twist your wrist like the trunk of an elephant in order to get the gravy from the most difficult corner, or go without. But the fertile mind of Ablard Pender invented a little hollow in the most convenient corner on such dishes, the corner I called north-west, and waiters can see this hollow and they let the gravy run there, so that a diner can get it without contortions. It may seem a trifle, but one firm saw the millions of little facilities that this would bring to diners, and bought Pender's patent. And that was another of the things that brought him in money. I asked one or two at the United if he had been seen, but they told me not. And then one day while I was there he came into the club. There was rather a radiant look about him, and, seeing me in the reading-room, he came straight up to me, singling me out, I think, because he must have considered that I was the one who showed the most interest in what he wanted to talk about, which was of course that brain of his.

"I've given it legs," he said.

"How many?" I asked, as I had of the hands.

"Four," he said. "It can run about like a dog."

He was evidently much excited by his success, from which I gathered that he had only just completed it, which turned out to be the case. And I think that this was the reason that he came up to the club, in order to talk about his iron brain, and I was the one that was to hear of it.

"It is wonderful," he said. "It is running about. I have given it four perfect legs. Rather like those of a crab, but of course much larger, and it can run a good deal faster than a crab."

"What are its feet like?" I asked.

"Pincers," he said. "What you would call claws if it was an animal. Just like a crab's. I find the hook-form more convenient than anything else, because it can pick up things."

"And are you still playing chess with it?" I asked.

"No," he said, "I have set it to work."

"What are you making it do?" I asked.

"I am leaving it very much to itself," he said.

"And what does it like doing?" I inquired.

"Making wires," he said. "Fine wires like what it is itself made of. It spins them all day. I have given it some little furnaces and plenty of coke and scrap-iron; and it melts the iron, and runs off the wires. You should come and see the ovens that I have got for it. I have rented a tumble-down cottage and an acre of land in the Thames marshes, and I take it down there in a taxi and let it run about, and it always goes straight to the ovens and stokes them up and melts the iron and goes on making the wires."

"But can it stoke a furnace?" I asked.

"Good lord," he said, "it's a lot cleverer than you or I. Its only limitation was locomotion. But, now I have given it legs and hands, it can do pretty well anything."

Well, as I have already said, there are always a good many members in our club, and some of them came up and we got talking of other things, and then I went to lunch. But although I saw no more of Pender that day, I thought a good deal of what he had said, and could not easily get out of my mind the picture of this crab-like creature of iron, cleverer than a man, running about on its own in the marshes of the Thames and stoking furnaces and making fine wire. And what did it mean to do with the wire? And was it really cleverer than man? If so—if so, we were no longer the greatest of created things. But could it be so? The awful thought it gave rise to, of mankind dropping to second place in the world, impelled me to go further into the matter. I don't think that the awfulness of the situation, if Pender's claim were true, had occurred to anyone else at the United. The possibility of mankind dropping to second place had never occurred to any of them, so that they could not be frightened into fearing that anything could bring about such a situation. Certain hints, certain warnings, had been coming to me for some time; for I had watched the increasing power of machines, seeing them firstly driving countrymen out of the villages to work in factories in towns, and then seeing them gradually dominate our very fancies, until artists began to paint in straight lines, which are almost unknown in nature and are the very essence of the machine, and architects began to build houses that were like packing-cases for machinery, with all the little human fancies gone, and no more decoration of leaves or wings, or any curves at all. These things that I had observed for some years were no more than forebodings, but they helped me now to see that something strange was afoot, and the little I knew of geology made me wonder if this might be the next in the long succession of those that have dominated the planet, of whom Man is the present heir.

CHAPTER II

I WENT back to the United next day and sat in the reading-room all the afternoon, hoping to see Ablard Pender, for I was still uneasy about the possibilities of his invention. I read all the evening papers without remembering much of the news, and as the afternoon wore away my uneasiness seemed to increase. And then about five o'clock in walked Pender, looking very jubilant, and I saw from a glance at his face that the power in which he rejoiced, and which I was beginning to dread, had made some further increase. Again he came up to me, and this time the first thing that I said was: "Could you show me your brain?"

He was delighted that I should take so much interest in what he was doing, and said at once that he would show it me, and I apologized for having made the suggestion, and he brushed my apology aside.

"Come and see it any time," he said. "I'm at Kingston Hill. Why not come and dine with me tonight?"

When I saw that he really meant it, I accepted.

"Don't dress," he said. "Come as you are. I live there with my aunt, and we haven't dressed for dinner since the war."

"One moment," I said. "I think I ought to tell you that I don't look on machines in quite the way you do. I don't want to argue against you, but I think it is only fair to say that I don't quite take your view that the work of machines will mean more leisure for men, because I think it has been rather the other way about."

"Perhaps in the past," he said. "But I don't think you quite realize that my machine doesn't need a man to look after it. It runs about on its own and works on its own, and any little difficulties that may have to be solved, which would normally be placed before the head of the firm, it works out for itself. So you see——"

13

"Yes, I see," I said. "But I thought it only fair to warn you."

"Well, you'll come and dine," he said.

So, with my warning only half given, I accepted his invitation. And some time after tea we started off together in the bus that takes you to Kingston Hill, and right past his garden gate. In the bus we talked about his little house and his aunt, and I rather gathered that she disapproved of her nephew for wasting his time with science, instead of being a chartered accountant as his father and grandfather had been.

"Don't you find it rather lonely, living there with just an aunt," I said after a while.

"Well, as a matter of fact," he said, "as a matter of fact," but at that moment somebody who had boarded the bus wanted to look at our tickets, and Pender said no more for a while. We had come to hedgerows at last, and a little breeze that was running beside the bus made all the wild roses wave to us, for it was early June.

"You were saying," I said, "that you lived all alone with your aunt."

"As a matter of fact," he said, "I wasn't thinking of doing that always."

"Not?" I said.

"No," said he. "As a matter of fact there's a girl. But we aren't engaged or anything, and I wouldn't like you to get the idea that we are, or to tell anyone there is anything in it. Only there is this girl, quite extraordinarily pretty, and really wonderful in every way, as you couldn't help seeing if you saw her. What I thought was— But it's no use talking of that when nothing is arranged."

"No, of course not," I said. "But I hope everything will come out all right."

"Well, I hope it might," he said.

And we rumbled on past hedges and woods and houses and streets and gardens, and came to Kingston Hill. In a little sandy bank in which were stray plants of harebells not yet in bloom, was his open garden gate. We went in together, and before he introduced me to his aunt, or went into his house at all, he took me to the old stable that was his garage and showed me his invention. It was crouched in a corner, and was obviously pleased to see him; but I didn't like the way that it looked at me, if looked is the right word, which perhaps it is not, for if it had eyes at all they were nothing like ours, but it was certainly aware of my presence, and it turned towards me at once with a very alert look. I suppose I stepped back a little; for Pender said to me: "Don't mind it."

Then he began talking to it, and it crawled back to its corner from which it had run out a little. It was a round shape of steel, inside which of course must have been the delicate wires which when stimulated by faint electric currents could move the stouter bars and hooks that were its arms and hands and legs, and the process whereby those nerve-like wires moved those iron limbs was thought. Of course I never saw any of the fine wires; they were inside the steel skull. A crab the size of a big dog was the rough description of it that first ran through my mind, but it was a quite inadequate description. Then Pender went out of the garage and turned towards his house.

"Hadn't you better lock the door?" I asked.

"As you like," said Pender. "But I have a perfect trust in it."

And to please me he locked the door. I was glad he did so; for I did not trust that thing with a hundred hands myself. I had only seen it for a few seconds, but I took one of those instinctive dislikes to it, that people say are unfair, and yet one cannot well help being guided by them. This was not a reasoned dislike. I had that already. It was an irrational dislike, arising from the mere look of the thing, and after only a single glance. Totally irrational, as I admit; and, as I must also admit, having more influence on me, a reasonable being, as I like to think myself, than the dislike I had formed with perfectly good reason. When I look at some of the things that people do I sometimes find myself doubting if *homo sapiens* is a fair description of us, and it is little influences like this in myself that nearly clinch my doubt. Yet I was not thinking of things like this now, or reasoning anything at all, but was merely dominated by an eerie feeling that sent little chills through my being and presentiments through my brain. Pender suddenly stopped in our walk to his hall-door.

"One thing," he said, "if you don't mind. I've never said a word to my aunt about this thing being alive. She knows all about it otherwise, and thinks it rather silly, but she doesn't know it's alive. If you wouldn't mind not saying a word that would let her see that——"

"Oh, certainly not," I said.

"Thank you very much," said Pender. "She knows it can move and all that, but she thinks it's remote control. She doesn't know it's alive."

"I won't say a word," I said.

And so we went into the house and, turning to our left from a rather dingy little hall, Pender showed me into the drawing-room, in which his aunt was sitting in the daylight that lingered brightly in that long summer's evening. She received me with politeness because I was a guest, but I could see at once that she disapproved of me, because, being a friend of her nephew, I was immediately suspect of encouraging and abetting him to waste his time over science, which, being the principal interest of Pender's life, would naturally not be disliked by his friends, at any rate not as she disliked it. Yes, there she sat talking politely to me, and looking more austerely at her nephew, and disapproving of us both.

"I suppose my nephew has shown you his gadget," she said.

Whether she was trying to show that she was familiar with modern phraseology, or whether she thought she was using the correct scientific term, I never knew.

"Oh yes," I said, "I have just seen it."

"Couldn't you persuade him," she said, "to spend some of his time on more useful things."

"I will try," I answered.

I don't know how much money she had of her own, but I was sure that a great many of her comforts came from what her nephew had earned. Perhaps in the silence she saw me thinking of this, and she said: "I don't mind when he makes useful things, but that thing he keeps in the garage covered with claws doesn't look very useful, and must have cost more than what a young man ought to spend on his hobbies."

'Hobbies!' I thought, and for a moment the word brought a gleam of comfort. For what I had feared, with a fear that I hope was exaggerated, might threaten the supremacy of mankind, was to Mrs. Mary Ingle only a hobby.

Soon we went into the dining-room, and the conversation at dinner, so far as Mrs. Ingle directed it, seemed chiefly to tend to extol various occupations that a young man might take up which were not scientific. After dinner we went to walk in the small garden that sheltered under the wall of Richmond Park in the long glow of the evening and, passing the old stable on our way, a pawing and scratching from the machine was distinctly audible. I thought that the state of things must be clear at once to the aunt; but all she said was: "Ablard is always keeping that machine of his wound up. It must be a great waste of petrol, or whatever he runs it with."

"I will turn it off," said her nephew, and turned back while we went into the garden, and must have spoken to his machine; for, when we came back to the house in the last of the gloaming, everything was silent in the stable.

"Would you like a game of chess?" said Pender as soon as we got back to the house. I knew that he meant with the monster, but how he thought I could play chess with it without his aunt seeing that it was alive I could not imagine. I looked at him, and he saw what I was wondering about. "Oh, that will be all right," he said. So I said I would play. And Ablard Pender brought the monster in on a wheelbarrow. It could have quite easily walked. But that would have given it away to the aunt. Well, in it came in the wheelbarrow into the dining-room, because there was more room

B¹

there, and it kept perfectly still. He certainly seemed to have
it under as good control as any well-trained retriever. Then
he asked me to help him lift it on to the table, and I said I
would, but regretted it. It was like handling a horrible insect.
Luckily it still remained quiet. I could not have stood it if
it had started buzzing like a fly, or moved any of its arms
with their crab-like claws. The moment that we got it on to
the table I stepped back out of its way, and there the disgusting thing crouched with a chess-board in front of it,
put there by Ablard Pender, and his aunt never knew that it
was alive. At the other side of the board at the end of the
table Pender placed a chair for me. I sat down and set the
board. Still the disgusting thing never moved, but it was
evidently watching the board and me. One usually draws for
white and first move; but I just took white, and let the thing
protest if it wanted to: I didn't see how it could: nor did it.
I played that complicated opening, the Ruy Lopez, assuming
and, as it turned out, quite rightly, that with all the work that
Pender had had to make those hundred hands and four legs,
he would not have had the time to teach openings to the
monster and would have taught it little more than the rules.
So I played the Ruy Lopez and fancied that I should soon
have the thing out of its depth. But its answers led to involved
variations that I had never seen before and that, as far as I
have been able to find out, are in no books. Surely, I thought,
as it made its first move, gripping the king's pawn with one
of the crab-like pairs of its hundred pairs of claws, surely
now Mrs. Ingle must see that the thing is alive. But no. She
had heard, when she was young, of a chess-automaton that
used to play games at the Crystal Palace and win them. Of
course it was a fake; there was a chess-master inside the
image; but it had taken in the public and was enough for
Mrs. Ingle, and she believed that a machine could easily play
chess and that it was only a machine that was playing now.
It was watching me intensely, rather as a cockroach watches
one. You do not see a cockroach's eyes, but you know an
alert creature is keenly watching you. Once some movement

it made attracted Mrs. Ingle's attention and she looked rather carefully at it, but Pender was quick to divert her.

"I asked Alicia to look in this evening," he said, "if she is out on her bicycle."

"I don't like young girls cycling about so late on their own," said Mrs. Ingle.

"Why not, Aunt Mary?" he asked.

"Because they come to no good if they do," she said.

"But you won't mind her coming here?" said Pender.

"Oh no," said Aunt Mary. And she had forgotten whatever it was that had caught her eye in some movement made by the monster.

"How are you getting on?" she asked of me.

I was not getting on at all. I had realized, some moves back, that I was facing a superior intelligence. You find out that very quickly at chess. And I was suspecting pretty strongly that it was an intelligence superior to that of mankind. It may seem that I had not had long in which to come upon such an astonishing suspicion; but chess is a convenient testing-ground, and when, applying that rough-and-ready test, I found that something that had had only a few lessons could invent a variation to the Ruy Lopez that I had never seen in any book, then that was the extraordinary suspicion that began to arise in my mind. So I replied guardedly to Mrs. Ingle, remembering my promise to Pender not to let his aunt guess the truth; and she, seeing that my answer was vague and that my vagueness was deliberate, searched at once for my motive and found the wrong one. She thought, quite rightly, that I was losing the game, and wrongly that that was what I had hoped to conceal. And then the doorbell rang and there was Alicia, the young girl that Pender had told me about, with her bicycle leaning against the porch and her lamp not yet lit, as we saw through the window of the dining-room when Pender turned out the light for a moment in order to see outside. This left the dining-room nearly in the dark, which added a sinister touch to the monster crouched on the table, and I was glad when Pender turned

on the light again, before running to the hall-door to let in
Alicia. Alicia was a charming girl, fresh from the beauty
parlour that has no rival on earth, the one kept in the open
air by old Dame Nature. There was a flush in her cheeks
and a light on her lips that Rubens could never have equalled,
and no painter had tried to improve what paint could only
have spoiled. The phrase that came to my mind as I saw her
was the ungilded lily, but actually I thought of a wild rose.
Her figure was slender, and graceful as that of many young
girls, but her lips were lovelier than any that one sees now.
Yet I will not take time to describe her, for three things
caught my attention now like flashes of lightning. First of
all, though that was a mild flash, like summer lightning
among louring clouds, there was Mrs. Ingle's polite reception
of Alicia, politer even than her reception of me, but with a
cold light that seemed to glow in her eye. I cannot describe
it. She received Alicia as a hostess should; and yet at the
same moment something told me that she did not want
Alicia to be the mistress of that house. That was one flash.
The next one came like forked lightning from Alicia. She
saw at once as she entered the room that the monster was
alive.

I spoke of two flashes of lightning, two appreciations that
came suddenly before my eyes, instead of being worked out
by the experience sometimes of years. One may know people,
for instance, for a long time, and one day one may say to
someone: "I rather think that Mrs. Ingle does not want
young Pender to marry Alicia Maidston." I saw that in a
single flash. Then Alicia instantaneously saw what I said.
But I mentioned three flashes. The third was more like
thunder. And I may say that the echoes of it jar in my mind
to this day, and shall do all my life. Looking back on all the
awful things I have seen, I put this as the first. I cannot tell
you how I perceived it, only that, as clearly as I saw in Mrs.
Ingle's eyes that she did not welcome Alicia, I saw in the
attitude of the crouching thing against which I was playing
chess that it was jealous of Pender's girl. Alicia Maidston

stood gazing silently at the monster, and it ostentatiously
made a move on the board, a move that was a good deal
too deep for me. Then Pender said to the girl: "What do
you think of it, Alicia?"

Still Alicia stood silent. In those moments, that were
probably fewer than what I thought, her gaze seemed to
roam as far as dreadful influences that this machine might
have on the story of man. Then she answered Pender's
question by parrying it with another. "Did you make it
entirely yourself?"

"Yes, of course," said Pender. "Don't you like it?"

"Time will have to show that," said she.

Time. What had that gaze of hers seen, when it seemed
to be peering into the future? I was introduced to her then,
and she said: "Do you find it clever?"

"Too clever for me," I said.

"I was afraid so," said Alicia.

"But what are you worrying about, Alicia?" blurted out
Pender.

"Did I say I was worried?" asked Alicia.

"No," said Pender, "but you looked it. What is
wrong?"

"Nothing is wrong here," she said. "It was the future
that I was looking at."

"Looking at the future?" said Mrs. Ingle. "Whatever
did you see?"

"Nothing," said Alicia. "It was too dark."

Mrs. Ingle merely stared at her. So did Ablard Pender;
but he stared with admiration, seeing something in Alicia's
vision which his aunt thought merely absurd, and which
Alicia herself admitted was only a gaze into darkness, something that to him seemed to add to the wonder with which
he obviously regarded Alicia. Then Ablard Pender went up
to the monster with a clock key in his hand and pretended to
wind it up, so as to conceal from his aunt what it really was;
but he did not deceive Alicia. She said very little and continued to look at the monster, and from time to time lifted

her gaze to thoughts that I could not follow. And, watching
Alicia, the uneasiness that I had felt already became more
acute, and, as I rapidly lost my game against the monster,
I wondered more and more what Alicia saw in the future,
and I feared for the race of man.

CHAPTER III

THERE is not much more to say about my visit to Sandyheath, which was the name of Ablard Pender's house. I lost
my game of chess. I lost it utterly. But it was a very interesting game, and I wish I had kept a record of it, for I think
that there were moves in it, though none of them made by
me, that were more profound than any that have been
played as yet in the Ruy Lopez. And I wish I could quite
remember all the moves that the monster made, for I believe
that, if I could, nobody would be able to win who played
the Ruy Lopez against me, an opening that chess-players who
have the first move are very likely to play. I was of course
astonished by the game, but Mrs. Ingle saw nothing odd in
it and never guessed the presence in her dining-room of an
intellect superior to anything human. She was more interested
that evening in trying to pump me about her nephew's
frequent journeys to the Thames marshes, when he went
away with his new invention in his car. She seemed to want
to know to what part of the marshes he went, and what he
was doing there. And there were so many things about that
that I did not know myself, that it was easy for me to keep
my promise to Pender, and much of the time to be perfectly
frank. We both made several guesses, but that the thing was
alive never occurred to her; though there it sat with its
jealousy of Alicia smouldering to glowing hatred. It is hard
to describe how it showed it, though unmistakable when one
has seen it, as it is with the jealousy of a dog. I think that
Mrs. Ingle's curiosity as to what her nephew did in the

marshes made me curious too, and when he saw me that
night to the bus that was to take me back to London I asked
him if he would let me see what his invention was doing
there. I said that I thought his machine was perfectly wonderful, and that I would like very much to see it at work. Pender
agreed to take me to the marshes and show me the thing
working, and I thought he would agree eagerly, for he was
naturally proud of his extraordinary invention, and of being
able to make it work, which is a great deal more wonderful
than merely getting the idea of it. But Pender did not agree
eagerly. Gladly enough, but not eagerly; for his eagerness
seemed to have gone. What it seemed to me now was that
Pender was no longer triumphant, but was glad to have me
with him in a different capacity. He had brought me to
Sandyheath to admire his cleverness. And why not? Admiration was due to him, and he was not going to get any from
his aunt, and Alicia he thought was not sufficiently in touch
with science to understand; though, remembering the look
on her face when she saw the machine squatting in front of
me as I tried to play the Ruy Lopez, I thought she saw far
further into the thing's possibilities than ever its inventor
was able to do. As for the men at the club, they had their
own affairs to consider, without bothering about what a
young scientist might be doing, or thinking very much about
science at all. But now it seemed, as we walked in the dark
past his rhododendron on my way to catch the last bus,
he was no longer in need of my admiration, but wanted
someone to be with him in those marshes, rather as we like
to have someone with us in some dark corridor, if without
them we should be all alone by night in a house believed
to be haunted. That was what I fancied, as we saw the lights
of the bus. He seemed anxious that I should come with him
to the marshes to see his invention at work, but no longer
jubilant about it. He may have seen from the thing's mastery
of the Ruy Lopez that there was something there beyond
what he had foreseen, or some reflection from the face of
Alicia may have chilled his mind with its first fear. His vast

intellect, quite unrecognized by his aunt, had been wholly occupied with daily details, the little things that would make his monster work, hundreds of them and even thousands, a delicate wire to be put into position and fastened, the little supply of electricity that would animate it, details smaller and more numerous than I ever knew, completely filling his time; but a young girl had leisure to look into the future, and I believe that what she saw there was far beyond Pender's dreams. Even now, influenced by Alicia's forebodings as no doubt he was, I think he was blind to certain possibilities whose outlines to Alicia were clear. And those possibilities were threats to the human race.

We fixed the following day for our journey down to the marshes. Pender was going to put the thing in a box and bring it to the club in his car, and pick me up and go on to where the furnaces were, at which his monster worked with its hundred hands, about a mile over the marshes beyond the old man's cottage, melting iron and spinning delicate wires all day. All the way back to London I pictured the thing at work. I thought of a thing with the industry of a spider and the brains of Capablanca at work on a modern factory. I thought of all that we were able to do with our machinery, worked by no more than ordinarily skilled men working seven hours a day with a day and a half off each week. What might these very machines be able to do, I wondered, if worked by genius twenty-four hours a day year after year? Well, my speculations were not of interest, and they were dulled by a certain fear.

Next day I was waiting at the Schools United at the time Pender had fixed, and he walked in and we had tea together. Somebody made a joke about Frankenstein's monster, the creature of fiction invented by Shelley's wife, a joke that was now the property of the club and that was usually handed out to Pender when he came into the room, and which served as well as 'Good morning'. I sat rather silent during that tea, because I wanted to warn Pender about what I had seen in the attitude of the monster, and the words would not easily come. And when a few words did come I suddenly realized how awful was the thing I was going to say; and I said no more than: "I was wondering about Miss Maidston."

"Yes?" he said.

But I could not go on with it. A machine! And yet alive! The thought was too horrible. And I was glad when another member came by and said: "What do you feed your Frankenstein on, Pender?"

"Oil," Pender replied.

"Shouldn't like it," said the other.

"Why not?" asked Pender.

"Sooner have whiskey," said the man and passed on, perhaps to get some.

After tea we went to where Pender had parked his car, with the box in it, and, arising from the box, no more than a slight hum. I sat in front with Pender, and the box was behind, and away we started through the most tamed part of the planet, where Mother Earth is held down by chains of pavement and kept in dungeons of brick; though the goal of our journey was an eternal thing, wild marshes where Earth was free.

Once more, during that journey I tried to warn Pender that the thing was aware of Alicia. But the words would not come. Evening was coming on. Suddenly houses ended; and we came to one of those great cabbage fields that feed London, haunted by whisps of night that strayed in the dimness of evening. It was a wonderful change from streets. And yet it was still a part of the wide dominion of Man. But beyond the brow of a little hill on which the cabbages grew there loured a bank of mist, and under that was land that owes no allegiance to us; under that lay the marshes. Men had been there too, as an old thatched cottage showed, but they came there as strangers, not as the masters of hundreds of orderly rows of cabbages, drawn up by Man, and to serve his needs in the end. And glowing there with all the splendour of flowers, as the evening darkened around it,

I saw the first of the furnaces that were tended by Pender's monster. Pender drove the car as far as the road would hold it, and where it became a track soon lost in water and rushes he stopped and opened the box and let the monster out. And it ran over marshes faster than any crab, straight for the glow of its furnace. I had not seen it run before, and the effect of it on myself was intensely horrible. I don't know why movement should have seemed worse than thought. I had seen it think deeper than I could, and now I saw it run faster, and this seemed the more horrible of the two. It splashed away over the marshes like a hare, and came splashing up to the furnace and crouched in front of it, and I saw the metallic monster glow in the light that streamed from the furnace door, a sight that was altogether horrible to me. Pender watched it without saying a word, with what seemed satisfaction at what he had made, but a satisfaction shot through with some new feeling that blew like cold winds on the other, as though the triumphant inventor looked for the first time at the future and found it haunted by something that he could not clearly see. Darkness deepened over the marshes as we stood there, and the glow of the furnace brightened, till most of its lovely colours were lost in the glare. And the thing took hold of some shovels and threw more coke into the fire.

I saw now, what had been hard to believe, that this intelligence, that had been proved over the chess-board to be so far superior to mine, was able to work a shovel and stoke a furnace. Why it should have been hard to believe I cannot think, but the fact remains that I was more surprised to see the monster doing a simple act with a shovel than I had been to see it outmoding one of the best-established openings at chess. We gazed silently at it stoking its furnace and throwing in bars of iron. As the glow of the furnace increased, an old man came towards us along a rushy track that led from the thatched cottage which we had passed on our way through the marshes.

"Ah, it's back at work, sir," he said to Ablard Pender.

"Yes," he answered and continued to gaze at his monster, dark in the glow of the furnace. A cold breeze began to wander over the marshes. I reflected on the splendour of ambition, and what a brilliant light it is in the lives of men, compared with any achievement. Here was one of the greatest inventions of our age, and the young inventor was gazing at it sadly, while fears and forebodings seemed to be haunting the marshes. And all because of a look on Alicia's face, as far as I could make out, and a new line of thought that that look had started, roaming into the dark of the future away from the calculations and wires and electric currents in which he used to delight.

"I kept all the furnaces alight for it, sir," said the old man. "It can see to them itself now."

"Yes," said Ablard Pender.

The old man was evidently in his employment, the furnaces were his, the piles of coke and the bars of iron and the land on which we stood, as well as the cottage in which he lived about a mile away.

He saw my eye roaming about his property and said: "I happened to make a good deal by a very simple invention. I sold a thing for picking up tennis-balls, merely a bamboo stick and a circle of rubber with a diameter the sixteenth of an inch smaller than that of a tennis-ball, and a muslin bag that would hold five or six of them. It was a simple little thing, but it brought me in enough to buy this bit of the marshes and have those furnaces built, and to buy the coke and the iron and to pay him to look after the property," indicating the old man. "And what they call my Frankenstein did the rest."

"Anything you want done with the furnaces?" said the old man.

"No, thank you," said Pender. "My machine will see to all that."

"Thank you, sir," said the old man. "Then I'll be getting home to my house."

And he took one look at the sky and the marshes, all

blending into one bleakness, and walked away to where his window glowed in the distance from below the dark of his thatch.

"We'd better see what it is doing," said Pender to me. And we walked over the wet and oozy ground the way that the monster had gone. Suddenly out of a tuft of rushes there got up a black thing in the gloaming and scurried away like a colossal beetle towards the glow of the furnace. I was chilled with horror, and before I could make out what the thing could possibly be, it became indistinguishable in the little light that remained, where it scuttled swiftly away from us. I stood there perfectly speechless.

"It's been making several of those things lately," said Pender.

"Good lord!" I exclaimed, "what things?"

"Things the same as itself," he said.

"But can it possibly do that?" I asked.

"I made it," said Pender. "Get into your head that it is cleverer than I."

"Then it can," I said.

"What I can do," said Pender, "it can do much better."

So there were several of these horrible things, and they were loose in the marshes. As we went on the glow of the furnace, increasing as daylight faded, illuminated our track, while black against that glow we saw the shape of the busy monster with most of its hands at work. I told how Alicia, simpler but far surer than Pender's aunt, saw at once that the thing was alive. Dogs too knew it at once, as I discovered by watching a dog that I saw coming away from the lonely cottage towards the monster, whose movement he must have seen in the glow; and when, ahead of us, it reached the path along which the monster had gone, it put its nose repeatedly to the ground and lifted it up again with a puzzled expression, and I realized that what was puzzling it was that this active thing that the dog had seen in the marshes was of all living things the only one that had no smell. Puzzled, the dog went on until it was close to the monster. Then it stopped and lifted its throat and uttered so awful a cry, that it might have warned us that Ablard Pender's invention was something fraught with horror to all whom nature had given the inner eye that can see, though even dimly, any outline of those forebodings that haunt the dark of the future. Once more the dog howled. And then Pender's monster came for it, scurrying over the marshes like a terribly magnified beetle, and seized the dog by the throat with some of its hands. The dog bit, but bit upon iron. And before we could do anything it had torn the dog to pieces and was holding the pieces up so as to let the blood run all over it. Its idea of eating, I suppose.

"I say, Pender," I said. "Is that quite right?"

"No," said Pender. "But what are we to do?"

"Couldn't you . . ." I began. But I saw the thing looking at me in the light of its furnace, and did not like to say more in its horrible presence.

"You saw what it did to the dog," I said to Pender as we walked away from the marshes where he had left his monster to its own devices.

"I know it is a very beastly thing," said Pender. "I see that now. But look what it will do for mankind. Look at the work it will save them, and at the leisure that it will give. Motors kill more dogs than that, and men, women and children too. But you wouldn't stop motors."

"It wasn't of that," I said, "that I wanted to talk to you. I was thinking about Miss Maidston."

"Alicia?" he said. "What has she got to do with it?"

"I saw the way it looked at her," I said.

"Looked at her?" said Pender. "What do you mean?"

And it was hard to explain what I meant, because there was a horror about the thing looking at the girl, that seemed to congeal my words. But I had to go on, since I had started. "I think it's jealous of her," I said.

That was a new idea to Pender. But wild as it may seem to my reader, Pender did not scoff at it, and thought for a while in silence. He knew that an intellect like that which had not only beaten me at chess, but had rolled up a time-honoured opening, was well able to understand, and probably with a single glance, what Alicia Maidston meant to him. And how would it, which obeyed every word of Pender's, care for one whom Pender was prepared to obey as devotedly, and for whom he cared far more than he cared for his monster? So I said: "I thought that I ought to tell you."

And I left him to his thoughts.

We drew near to the old thatched cottage, with the glow of its window falling upon our track, before I spoke again. "And what of that old man," I said, "all alone with them in the marshes?"

"He has to oil them," he said.

"Is he safe with them here?" I asked.

"I can answer for the one that I made," he said. "All the others seem all right too. But I'll tell him not to allow them to get too familiar with him."

CHAPTER IV

I DO not remember what I said to Pender any more that night. I think we walked to the car in absolute silence. And I think that all the way home I dwelt alone with my thoughts, which were darkened and even chilled by a strange idea, which Pender's words in the marshes had awoken. There was something now loose in the world which might get too familiar with men! That was the thought that filled my meditations with horror. I said nothing of it to Pender. For what could he tell me? He was no more than a carpenter who had made a queen for a chess-board. He could no more tell the effect his invention would have on the future than that carpenter could predict the courses of games of chess that would be played with the piece he had made. What inventor can?

As I sat silent in the car Pender was obviously aware that I was, to put it mildly, dissatisfied with his invention, and he spoke little either. This invention of his was the greatest achievement of his life, a thing not often surpassed in this age of inventions; but, had he spoken of it to me that evening, after what the thing had done to the dog, even leaving out the menace that I now saw it was to mankind, he must have been on the defensive. And so he was silent. No, he could have told me nothing. My own fears may have exaggerated, they may have run down many wrong turnings, but they could see into the dark of the future, in which these monsters prowled, as far as Pender could see.

Pender put me down at my flat, and I thanked him and said good night. I don't remember what more I said. And I went to bed still wondering about the future of Man, and what the effect on it of Pender's monster would be. I think I lay awake all night worrying over this, as people some-times do with small worries. But I was worrying over the fate of mankind. The central concern of my worry was simply this: could these things go on reproducing them-selves? Pender had told me they could. And I had seen one of them. Pender's monster could make others. Could these in their turn make more? If so, what limit would there be to it? In all zoology I knew of only one limit to reproduction, and that limit was the enemies of a species. What enemies would these iron monsters have? Were it not for their enemies, flies and even oysters could cover between them the surface of the planet. Indeed oysters had done so over large areas, for I had seen a layer of them many inches thick, just above where the chalk ended, which must once have covered some great space. That particular race of them had had its turn and ended. Would the same fate befall man? It seemed to me in the troubled hours of the night that it all depended on the powers of reproduction of these monsters that, so far as I could see, would find nothing upon this planet that would be able to check their growth, except Man. And it was about that exception that I troubled all night. Would the time come when Man's cleverness would get ahead of him, when the inventions that it had created would be too much for their creator? Had it come already? Our civilization was getting more and more complicated before Pender's time; more and more machines upon which we all depended were understood by fewer and fewer, as their intricacies increased. And now Pender's invention. Was this the thing that was to dethrone us, as Zeus dethroned Chronos?

Chronos and Zeus were myth, and these machines were reality; but all the old tales of the Greeks were so shrewdly told by men who had looked so clearly upon life, that they can guide us yet. Was a dominant regime, an old power, going to fall before its children now, man usurped by his own machines as Zeus usurped Chronos?

When light slipped into my room through chinks in the curtains, vague fears went away with the night, and reason shone in their places; and reason told me that I must find out what powers of reproduction these monsters had.

I got up early and, after breakfast, as early as I thought Pender would be up and about, I telephoned to him. I did not tell him on the telephone what I was worrying about; but, little although I said, he seemed to guess that I was uneasy. I merely asked him if he would take me again to his factory and let me see his employees at work. And he kindly said he would take me that afternoon, and when I thanked him he said that he had been intending to go in any case. We arranged a time to meet at the club. And there was Pender waiting when I arrived, and we set off in his car at once.

"How many of these other things is your machine making?" I asked, as we crossed the Thames and turned eastwards.

"I don't know," he said. "It makes as many as it likes."

"And can they make others?" I asked.

"I suppose so," he said.

"Where will it stop?" I asked.

"But I don't want it to stop," he answered. "They'll work for us. We shall have all the advantages of slavery without the harm of it."

"What advantages?" I asked.

"Don't you see," he said rather impatiently. "We shall start on a level of leisure higher than what we have known. Just think what you could do if you began the day with all the odd jobs of a household done. The human race will be like that, when all the tiresome work has been done for them by these machines. There will be opportunities we have never had before. We shall lift our civilization, because we shan't have to start at the bottom. Can't you understand what it will mean?"

"But do you quite like that thing you have made?" I asked him.

"It isn't a question of liking," he said. "The Americans did not bother about whether they liked their slaves. They just made them work."

"Yes, I see," I said, whatever I meant by that. And we went down two small streets before I said any more. And then I said: "I suppose you never allow it to be alone with Miss Maidston."

And he said: "I don't think there is any harm in it."

But though he had defended his monster against the human race, when I had suggested the thing was a danger to it, I saw by the look in his eyes that he thought more of Alicia than of the monster that he had made, and that my fear for her safety had communicated itself to him. So there was no more that I needed to say. And I sat silent for the rest of the journey, wondering what I should see when we got to our destination. We did not go by the road by which we had gone last time, which ended with a walk through the marshes past Eerith's hut, but went by one that took us by dry land almost up to the door of the sheds in which the furnaces were; for they stood at the edge of the marshes, across which we saw the thatch of Eerith's hut rising dark against the pale light of the desolate waste.

Pender and I left the car and went up to the door of the shed, which Pender opened and we went in, and I saw at once the monster that he had made crouched on the floor,

C

very busy, with the light from the door of a furnace glowing along its back, looking just like the horrible beetle that it had always seemed to me. It was at the far end of the shed and, as we walked towards it, I saw that it was pulling thin strips of metal through a hole in a bar of iron, clamped to a rough table. Pender explained to me that it was making wires. That bar of iron had apertures at the back, which narrowed to small holes of various sizes in front. The strips of metal were pointed, and when the point was inserted through the wider aperture behind the bar of iron it could be pulled out through the front of it. A man would have used pincers, Pender told me; but this thing was using its bare iron hands. As the metal was drawn forcibly through the minute hole in the front of the bar of iron it became a wire, its thickness depending on what hole it had been forced through, for there was a row of holes in the iron which were all of different sizes. I walked up softly, hoping not to disturb the thing, for I did not know what it might do; but Pender assured me that when at work it was quite absorbed, as it had been at that game of chess, and that we could walk straight up to it. And so we did, and the thing went on with its work, and I noticed that the wire that it was drawing through the iron bar was drawn through the smallest hole in the row. Lower down on the floor it was making something, some large shapeless lump of quantities of fine wire.

"Another brain," said Pender.

But what astounded me more than what it was making was the fact that it was busily doing that intricate work with some of its hands, while two others were making more wire. This astonished me and perturbed me. For, though there seems no reason why we should not work with two hands at once, it is nevertheless beyond our human powers to do any absorbing work with one hand, and something else at the same time with another. And from this I saw, what I had seen already over the chess-board, that I was in the presence of a superior intelligence.

It is not because we have only two hands that we cannot

do what this thing was doing. It is because our brains are unable to attend to any two pieces of careful work at the same time; and, though we had a hundred hands, we could not have done what the monster was doing now. With elaborate care it was putting the pointed end of a long thin rod of metal through the wide end of the hole in the iron bar, then gripping it with one of its iron hands and drawing it through with amazing speed. Others of its hands seized hold of the coils of wire, coiled them more neatly and passed them to yet more hands, and from them to the half dozen or more of the iron claws that were intensely occupied with convolutions of what must have been hundreds of yards of delicate wire, that were making the shapeless mass of what Pender told me was to be another brain. It was as though I had seen a dentist drilling a patient's tooth, working carefully close to the nerve, and with the other hand at the same time doing an etching. Such a thing is beyond human capabilities. It was terrible to see how easy its two occupations evidently came to the monster, and how rapidly and efficiently it was dealing with them.

As we stood there in silence and watched the monster working away without ever looking at us, I noticed, what I had not noticed at first, that the wire that it rapidly drew through the iron bar was not drawn through only one hole, but through as many as forty or fifty holes that there were in a long row, each one smaller than the one before, till the wire was as thin as a piece of wire could be. And sometimes the monster passed one of its wires into yet another of its hands, to be lowered into a fire that glowed in a pit beside it, and to be handed back as soon as it was red hot. This, Pender explained to me, was to soften the wire so as to prevent it breaking. It was strange to see it handling the glowing wire with its bare hands, for its awful vitality made it hard for one to believe that it was only iron. And then I saw other of its hands gripping a file and sharpening the ends of the iron rods that were to be pulled through the apertures to make wire; and once again I was dreadfully aware that I was watching something that Man could not do. It would be perfectly possible for instance to sharpen a pencil to a fine point with one hand, provided that either the pencil or knife were firmly clamped, but no man could do other careful work at the same time, as this thing was doing continually. The sun was low at the time and light in the shed was dim, and the huge curved back of the monster glowed in the light that rose from the fire beside it, which burned in a little pit that was sunk in the floor, and from which a small tunnel ran to a chimney of brick.

The shed, to its dimmest recesses, was untidy with work upon which the monster had been engaged. Crucibles, great thick tubs that were made of graphite, lay about everywhere, with dregs of various metals littering the bottoms of them, like old tea-leaves in an untidy tea-pot, and bowls lay about on trestles, that seemed at first glance to be filled with gold, but which actually contained shavings of bronze. What it had been making with bronze I do not know, probably limbs for the other monsters; but it was evidently making a brain now out of those delicate wires, and it began to take some kind of shape as we watched. Then one of the monsters that it had made ran in and scurried the length of the shed, and out at the far end. Large cobwebs hung on the wall by which it ran, grey with old dust, and the sight of them and the shape of the thing that hurried past set me thinking of spiders, and their strange delicate work, of which we know nothing. How many creatures there are besides us in the world! And how little we know of their work! And here was yet another; something that had not been before, something that was not intended. What was its work, I wondered? I supposed that it filled the crucibles that I saw lying about, and lowered them into the furnace beneath the floor, while the monster that had made it did the delicate work that it was now doing with those fine wires along which were to run those impulses such as run along nerves through our brains. One crucible that perhaps had been dropped by some careless monster was broken and its bright edges shone like lead, very different from lead though they were, for lead melts almost instantly in a furnace, and this bright graphite would never melt at all, with bronze bubbling within it. The monster that worked at the brain had not yet noticed us. But then Pender broke the silence in which we had stood watching, and the moment he spoke to me the monster looked up. Dog-like, at the sound of his voice, it seemed to expect some order; but Pender gave it none, and all of the iron hands that it was using went busily on with their work. All Pender said to me was what I had already guessed, that the monster we had just seen scurry away was one of those that did the menial work for the horrible thing he had made. Now that the monster had obviously noticed us, I was more than ever eager to get away. I saw that the thing had some slave-like kind of devotion to Pender, but there in its horrible home, with its other monsters around it or hurrying by, I did not know what it might do to me if Pender's interest should be distracted for a few moments among all the strange apparatus with which he had furnished his foundry. Any of the strange things lying there among dust and cobwebs might well attract his attention, and I found that I could not forget the fate of the dog.

"Perhaps we interrupt its work," I said.

"No, no," said Pender cheerfully.

I would have moved away then by myself, but that I did not want to be alone in that shed; but at least I got Pender to come a little away from the monster, by attracting his attention to a second furnace, that I saw glowing farther off in the shed.

"What has it got there?" I asked.

"There's iron melting in that," said Pender, "to make the shield on one of their backs. The others can do that."

And I got him to walk over with me to where the furnace filled another hole in the floor. Huge iron hooks that Pender had evidently bought to pull the crucibles out of the furnace stood leaning against a wall. But just then two more of the monsters came running up and, as I edged away, they pulled the crucible out with their bare hands, and the red-hot iron within it rippled like soup as they set the crucible down.

I had seen enough of these monsters' triumphant materialism, though the question I came to solve remained unsolved: could these monsters that Pender's monster had made make others complete, in their turn, or were they like mules? Pender did not know for certain. He only knew they could make the iron shields for their backs, and their legs and their claws, and that they could draw wire; but, whether it was that they kept it secret, or that they could not do it, he had never seen any of them making a brain, except his own monster. The two monsters crawled away with their molten iron, holding it up between them, to beat it into a shield for the back of the new one, Pender told me, and his own monster went on making bundles of nerves out of fine wire and shaping them into a brain much larger than any of ours. At last I got Pender to come away. As we walked through the shed, lit by the glow of the furnaces at the far end, and at the other dusty and cobwebbed, and dim except where the glow of a furnace shone on a hammock of cobweb, I asked him again about the abilities of these monsters, and got nothing more definite from him. But as we passed by a quantity of empty sacks that were heaped on the unswept floor, we saw one of them stir slightly, though no more than a rat would have stirred it, and Pender picked it up to see what was there. And there, all covered over with several sacks, was one of the monsters that his monster had made; and the problem was solved. For with long coils of wire that it had secreted among the sacks it was doing just what we had seen the parent monster do, and was obviously making a brain. The rest would be easy. The great shield for the back would be only hack-work, and the limbs would work easily enough once the brain was there to control them. So the monsters could do it. They could reproduce. And what chance would there be for men, when the planet was overrun by this new thing? I could see that the monster resented being observed, for with a sideways flick of its head, as quick as the movement of any insect, it looked up at Pender. He was in deadly peril. But he stood still in that cold metallic glare with so much the air of the master, as he was, of all these horrible things, that a certain awe of him seemed to abate the monster's anger. Then after that silent moment he moved away and threw back the empty canvas sack as he did so, leaving the monster to its work. I was very glad when we reached the open air and saw the twilight shining on natural things again, on the waste of water and rushes and a few green plover floating above them and crying, and the dark line of Eerith's thatch and the yellow glow of a light that suddenly winked from his window.

"So they can do it," I said to Pender.

"Well, I always thought they could," he said to me.

"But now you are sure?" I said.

"Yes, I am sure now," he replied.

"Then what's to be done?" I asked.

"Done?" said Pender.

"Yes," I said. "Their cunning is greater than ours. What will happen when their numbers are?"

"Their numbers?" he said. "But they won't make as many as that."

"What is to stop them?" I asked.

I am not wishing to exhibit any foresight of mine. I have no claim to any, for the situation was obvious. It is the blindness of Pender that I present to my reader, the blindness of the inventor who saw brilliantly the work under his hand at the moment and saw nothing at all of the path along which it would lead mankind. Then the yellow light of Eerith's distant window, that had briefly bloomed like one bright flower in all the wide garden of the marshes, blinked out, and his dark thatch frowned against the light water. I had forgotten Eerith. But soon I saw a figure that I knew must be his, coming in our direction.

"Is that Eerith?" I asked Pender, to make sure.

"Yes," he said. "He comes to oil them each evening."

"They can't oil themselves, then?" I asked.

"They can't possibly make oil," he said. "I have bought some drums of it, and given them to Eerith."

So they still had some need of man.

Far away over the marshes though Eerith was, and barely visible in the twilight, and though it must be long before the sound of his footsteps could possibly be audible to any human ear, yet there was a stir among all the monsters, both those that we had seen in the foundry and others that roamed or squatted outside. For we heard a sound of their iron limbs moving all at once, and they came out of the shed and from all round it, with their heads all pointing towards Eerith's cottage and seeming to gaze at him coming through the dim light, far away though he was. For a moment I thought that the whole herd of them was coming to attack us, for we were between them and Eerith; but then they all stopped and seemed to be peering anxiously.

"They are waiting to be oiled," said Pender to me.

I had little doubt now that they could conquer the world, with Eerith to help them, for they were cleverer than we and practically invulnerable. But could they make an obedient slave of Eerith? If not, I was afraid they could get others. Have we not enslaved elephants, let alone horses and cattle?

"You said that they could not make oil," I said to Pender.

"No, of course not," he answered.

"But could they not bore for it?" I asked.

"Possibly in some countries," Pender replied. "But I doubt it. And it mostly lies very deep. Certainly not in England."

It seemed to me that there was some hope in that, if they really needed oil. Then I asked Pender many more questions. But it was a profitless discussion, because, even if he perceived the danger of what he had done, still it was his own deed, and my questions drove him rather to defend it than to give me any hope for the future, whose complicated ways were all darkened by Pender's invention. The evening star had appeared, and its reflection lay like a silver lance in the water by the time that Eerith arrived. And there could be no doubt that the monsters were glad to see him. He carried a bucket half filled with oil, and he pulled a large rag from his pocket and dipped it into the oil and went up to one of the monsters and began to groom it all over, and all the others turned their heads his way as he did it. The monster that he was grooming showed the same kind of satisfaction that a dog shows when being combed and brushed, though it was far more like a huge beetle than any dog. I saw now that this was the hold that Pender had over them; but I wondered what they would have done to us, if they had not been waiting for their oil. One by one Eerith groomed them all, drying them first with a towel, if they had been splashed at all by the water that lay round the foundry, and then oiling them carefully, as any machine is oiled. Docile as they were during this oiling I would not have trusted one of them, and I felt like a man in a cage full of tigers, accompanied by a tamer of wild beasts and wondering sometimes at the extent of his influence over them. I was glad therefore when Eerith had oiled the last of them and turned at once to walk by his oozy track through the marshes back to his supper, and the monsters turned and all went back to their work. Pender looked round at them as though wondering what of their strange work he would show me next; and I took the opportunity of thanking him for all he had showed me, and when he offered to show me more I declined to trouble him further. So we left that strange place that was haunted with so much that I felt might trouble the world, and I was glad to see the wholesome lights of the streets again as we drove back to London and to hear familiar sounds, which, even if they were the sounds of machines, were of machines that could not yet dare to challenge mankind, however much they may threaten us.

CHAPTER V

IT was late when we got back to London, and yet when Pender rather perfunctorily asked me if I would not come into the club and have a drink I accepted, because I wanted to talk to him about certain risks with which I feared he was threatening mankind, and to suggest to him once again that a danger menaced Alicia.

But of neither of these things was he at all willing to speak, being held back from talk of the first by pride, which prevented him from admitting that anything but gain could come to us all from what he had done, and from the second by fear. What I feared, and at least indicated when I spoke to him, he would not speak of at all, but we each had the same fear. Things being like that, I soon finished my whiskey, and thanked Pender for the outing and went home to bed. It was some days before I saw Pender again in the club, and when I saw him he seemed very excited.

'What new marvel can he have invented?' I wondered.

He was standing at the far end of the reading-room, and several other members were talking with him. And then I saw that it could not, after all, be some great invention; for the other members of the Schools United were not that much interested in his work, and this was something that evidently attracted them. I walked up to the little group that there was round Pender, and got the news. He was engaged to Alicia. Of course I congratulated him, and very sincerely, for Alicia was a charming girl. And then he told me that it had all become suddenly possible, through the sale of another patent. For he had spent so much money over his monster and the furnaces he had had built for it that, sure though he was of earning all the money he wanted, his capital was only his brains, which even his aunt did not recognize, so that he could scarcely expect the girl's mother to do so. But about this time, stimulated perhaps by love, he invented his master-piece, which not only brought him in money enough, but placed him among the great benefactors of the human race. Like most of his inventions it was simple, but nobody else had thought of it. He knew that in the houses of England alone there were millions of square yards of oil-cloth, and that most of this area was thoroughly polished every day; and he realized that millions of men and women endured the risk to limbs and even to lives incurred by frequent falls on that dangerous surface. Others, he knew, told housemaids to do nothing dangerous to the oil-cloth; but he knew they told them in vain. Therefore he had invented a simple powder made mainly of sand and gum, which without the trouble of endurance, or of uttering requests that would never be heeded, could be thrown easily on to the oil-cloth to save many broken limbs. This simple and beneficient invention had made it possible for him to set aside money that would support Alicia whatever happened to him; and the only two ambitions that I knew him to possess were realized, one to marry Alicia, the other to free mankind from the drudgery of labour, and to give to the human race a leisure from which our civilization should be led to higher levels. Both these ambitions were of course of the future, but he saw them both close, and already to him they seemed realized. It is not often that any young man comes so near two such ambitions together, so near that he can see them shining upon his path and brightening it all the way into distant years. It is not I that say he was going to bring leisure to our race: I think that we have too many machines already, and that they have belied our hopes. I only record the happy ambitions with which his eyes were shining, and of which Pender was so sure. I did not like to mention the monster in the same breath with Alicia; but he did, and he told me that he had it at home in his garage.

"What of the others?" I asked.

"Oh, they're running about in the marshes," he said, "and doing no harm there."

I made no answer to that. And then he asked me to come down to Sandyheath again, and I accepted eagerly, and yet not gladly, for there was something horrible to me in the idea of Alicia and the monster so near each other, although I wanted to see the outcome of Pender's two infatuations that were more different than any two women have ever been who sought the heart of one man. It was then about three, and he told me that he was going down in his car in half an hour, and that Alicia would be there with his aunt, and that he would bring me down to tea that day if I liked. I jumped at the offer, as I looked forward to seeing Alicia again, for there was something about her that I felt would charm away my uneasy forebodings about the increasing power of machines, as a fresh breeze from the downs might blow away the fog of a city. He had given Alicia a motor bicycle, he told me, a thing I was glad to hear; for, whether or not such a machine seemed suited to Alicia, I knew that while she had that she could always outpace the monster, if it should chance to come on her alone and ever try to pursue her. So away we went westwards in Pender's car, and on the way down he told me of yet another of his inventions, which did not bring him in very much money, because it was not of general use; but all big hospitals bought it, and a few private individuals for reasons they never divulged. It, also, was simple. Merely a device for switching off a wireless set from another room and switching on to it instead the sounds of a gramophone playing in that same room, just as you can switch a wireless set off from whatever it is giving you and on to a gramophone playing a record that you have chosen, when wireless and gramophone are combined, as they often are. That was simple enough to understand, the moment he told me about it. What I did not understand at once was the use of it. And that I asked him.

"It has a very limited use," he said. "But nearly all the hospitals are buying a set. I only get a few shillings on each, but it all helps. Its use is that whenever they got a distinguished patient about whom the Press and the B.B.C.

wanted bulletins, the doctors had to write them in such a way that the public would be told how bad he was without alarming the patient, who would be sure to demand to hear the bulletin on the wireless and read what the papers said of his case. Not an easy thing to do. And of course if the nurses refused to let him hear the wireless or read the papers, then he knew he was dying. Now, with my invention all they have to do is to get the announcer of the B.B.C. to give a much more hopeful bulletin for a recording, and the record is sent to the hospital and put on a gramophone there and switched on to the wireless set at the right time on top of the real news. Same voice, and the patient suspects nothing. Then when he's heard all the news on the wireless the nurses find it quite easy to keep the papers away from him. It brings me in a little. As a matter of fact it about covered the motor bicycle that I got for Alicia."

At the mention of Alicia I thought of the monster again and asked Pender why he had brought it back to Sandyheath.

"I wanted to oil it," he said. "It gets all wet in those marshes. Of course I couldn't afford to buy a bit of land anywhere near London that wasn't marshy. Land you can possibly build on is worth hundreds of pounds an acre. And there would be people about. I don't want to have people about where I've got my machines. So it had to be marshes. But it's very wet for them. So I'm oiling it now."

"And what about the others?" I asked.

"That old man you saw looks after them," he said. "They have quite taken to him."

And I saw that for the monster that he had made, himself, he had some special affection, and would not trust anyone else to look after it. In past his little rhododendron we went, and Pender drove the car straight to the garage, and there I saw his monster crouched in a corner. It turned quickly towards Pender as he opened the door, and I noticed for the first time that it had eyes, two minute crystals, like those that are used for wireless, set in the front of the beetle-like skull of iron. Whether it was pleased to see its master or not I could not say, but it certainly had an eager look. I was glad to see that he locked the door when he left, and we went to the house and into the drawing-room, and there was Alicia. Mrs. Ingle received me, and I congratulated Alicia. And as soon as I could bring the conversation round to it I asked Pender about his kitchen-garden, and he jumped at the chance to go for a walk in it with Alicia, away from his aunt. For of course the aunt did not want to see her kitchen-garden, and I dropped off when we were half-way there, and strolled back to the house, making one of those excuses that you hear in a bad play. I walked slowly, having no real reason to go at all, except to leave Alicia and Ablard to themselves, and as soon as I got into the dingy little hall I heard voices from the drawing-room. I went slowly up to the door, hearing all that was said, and paused there wondering what to do; and then, seeing that I was obviously not wanted there, I turned away and strolled back to the door. And so I heard a good deal of what was said, and one of the voices was distinctly loud. The cook or the housemaid had evidently come into the drawing-room as soon as we left; and what I heard her say as I closed the hall-door was: "I understand human beings, and I understand animals."

And I heard Mrs. Ingle say: "A large claim, Eliza."

And then I heard the louder voice go on: "I understand everything God made; and it understands me."

And I made one of those coughs that one makes to let people know one is there; but it was drowned by the torrent of that voice which I heard continuing with the words: "And I like wholesome things."

"You haven't told me yet what it is that you don't like," said the calmer voice.

And the torrent broke out again: "I don't like things that Mr. Ablard makes."

It was about then that I came to the door of the drawing-room, but though I was nearer I could not hear the quieter voice of Mrs. Ingle. Perhaps she had heard my cough after all. I turned away then, and heard as I went some hurried allusion to something that had been done, and, rising to a louder pitch: "Do you think, mum, it can do that and run about by itself and beat people at games of chess if it isn't——"

"If it isn't what?" I think I heard Mrs. Ingle say.

"If it isn't——" said the loud voice again.

And Mrs. Ingle said: "Well?"

"Alive," said the other voice.

"Alive, Eliza?" I heard very clearly.

"Alive, I said," came the ringing answer, and I went out of the house.

CHAPTER VI

I WENT for a walk on the lawn in front of the house, if one can speak of a walk in such a narrow space. It brought me to the side of the old stables, now a garage, in which Pender's monster was kept, and I heard from it the kind of scratchings that one would hear from a beetle shut up in a box. I looked at the window and wondered if its latch would present much difficulty to an intelligent creature with all those hands; for, much as I had come to hate it, I had to admit that it was a very considerable intelligence. Soon I saw Pender and Alicia coming back to the house; so I returned to it too, and as I entered the drawing-room I heard Mrs. Ingle say to her nephew: "Either Eliza has gone raving mad, or. . . ."

And as I came in she stopped. But I saw from everything about her that the first shadow cast by the light of his genius was falling on Sandyheath. For there is no light without shade; and, though his aunt did not know it, the genius that was required for such an invention as made that living monster from wires and a sheet of iron was a very great light indeed, and was bound to cast shadows that were abnormally dark. And the first of these shadows was that his housemaid was giving notice. Alicia was not going to contradict Ablard Pender's aunt on her first introduction into the family, nor was she going to give any assent to the least disparagement of Ablard's genius; so she was silent and rather puzzled. Then Mrs. Ingle turned to her and said lightly: "Servants are very hard to keep these days. They will give notice for any trifle."

"She has given notice then?" said Pender.

"Yes," said his aunt, "that is what I was going to tell you."

"It will be very difficult to find another," said Pender.

And gradually the conversation rose from sinister chasms, to follow the lines of familiar domestic difficulties.

"Servants can be difficult sometimes. Can't they?" she said to me.

And I forbore to say that, if I were Eliza, I would not wait to give notice, but would go from that house at once. And somehow I saw from Alicia's face that those innocent words to me had even increased her knowledge that something was wrong, a knowledge she must have had since her first sight of the monster. What had kept that knowledge till now from Mrs. Ingle I could not imagine, unless it was the sheer force of her determination that her nephew could never do anything wonderful. But what she had not seen in the beetle-face of the monster she had evidently seen in the eyes of Eliza, and she was as uneasy now as some comfortable person in a warm arm-chair, who has suddenly gone to sleep and fallen into a nightmare. I think that she was quite honestly trying to warn Alicia of the menace that she had only just perceived, impending upon that house, when she said to her: "If Smergin were to give notice too, later on you might find it rather difficult."

"Oh, I could cook for Ablard and me, Aunt Mary," said Alicia.

So Smergin was evidently the cook, and Eliza must be the housemaid, and Mrs. Ingle's warning had fallen flat. She tried once again. "And then, if she and Eliza went, Ewens might go too," she said.

Ewens was their odd man, who looked after the garden and sometimes helped in the house.

"But why should Ewens go, Aunt Mary?" asked Alicia.

"If one of them gets some odd idea into her head, they might all get it," said Mrs. Ingle.

"An odd idea, Aunt Mary?" said Alicia.

And a door had slammed while they spoke, and we heard a step on the gravel, and there, past the drawing-room window, walked the cook with a bag in her hand, going away from the house. We watched in silence, till she came to the gate by the little rhododendron. Then Mrs. Ingle said to her nephew: "You see what you have done."

"Yes, I see that it must have frightened her," said Ablard Pender, "and I don't blame her. And it's inconvenient for us, her taking it like that. But science can't stop its progress for small inconveniences."

"Small?" said Mrs. Ingle.

"Well, not for any," said Pender. "We should have no trains, no artillery, no electric light, no anything, if that view had ever been taken."

And a certain exaltation seemed to have come upon Pender, with which neither his aunt nor Alicia seemed able to deal, and both of them looked at me. So, feeling I must not fail them, I joined in with the question to Pender: "But what if it brings disaster upon the human race?"

"Then the human race will have to endure it," said Pender. "But we can't stop science."

I looked at Alicia and Mrs. Ingle, and I saw that Alicia would not abandon Pender, however frightful his creed; while Mrs. Ingle, being unable to believe that her nephew could ever do much to the human race, was nowhere near as disturbed as I was. Both of them were uneasy, but neither of them realized the full horror of what Pender had said, and the whole of the shock of it was borne by me. In the silence that followed, the first words that were spoken concerned the difficulties that would trouble the kitchen of Sandyheath, and the rest of the conversation dealt with them, and nothing was said of the fate of the human race.

I wanted Pender to let the monster loose, so that they

D

could all see the way it looked at Alicia, and could draw their
own conclusions while we were there to protect her. But
Pender, however ready he was to let it loose on mankind,
was unwilling to risk Alicia. All of us in that house, now that
Mrs. Ingle's eyes had been opened by Eliza, were as well
aware that a menace was hanging chill over Sandyheath, as
butterflies or any other creatures are aware of a cloud that is
overcasting the sun. Only Pender, who alone might have
lifted the curse, was resolute not to go back on what he had
done, and Alicia would not withdraw her support from
Pender. I was only there as his guest. What could I do? Mrs.
Ingle alone resisted him. But she had thrown away the
influence she might have had, by never recognizing till now
that her nephew's work was anything out of the ordinary.
I shall always remember those moments in that drawing-
room, while nothing much was said, and I thought that the
best that I could do was not to stay for dinner, which Pender
had expected me to do, thus lifting from their shoulders the
only burden I could, which was the difficulty of feeding a
guest without a cook. What would happen I could not guess.
As I walked away from the door to catch a bus for London I
heard a rhythmic scratching coming from the old stables,
which gave me the idea that the creature was thinking. What
was it planning I wondered? But how could I tell that? It
had beaten me at chess, and my intellect was no match
for it.

CHAPTER VII

I HAUNTED the reading-room of the Schools United every
day for a week, hoping to see Pender again. But he did not
come to the club; and I wondered how things were going at
Sandyheath, with the cook gone and the housemaid giving
notice, and the odd man certain to know all that the housemaid knew. It was ten days before he turned up, and then I

came and sat down beside him and waited for him to talk, which he presently did.

"I've sent it back to the marshes," were the first words he said. And I gave a sigh of relief.

"Will your housemaid stay now?" I asked.

"She is not sure," said Pender.

Even that was something. And then I said: "What about the old man in the cottage? Are you sure that it will not harm him?"

"No. I have spoken to it," he said.

What he meant by that I had no idea, and I did not even ask him to try to explain.

"Is it still making more machines?" I asked him then.

But at that he grew secretive, as any man does if you ask him of the essentials of his business. But what I gathered from his vague answers was that, in the cause of science of course, he had invented a thing that could make machinery, and that to stop it doing that would be to set back the whole advance of science, which no man had the right to do, either with his own inventions or anyone else's.

"But supposing it makes a lot of them," I said.

"Then there will be all the more leisure for men," he replied.

And I knew it was no use arguing with him when in that mood. Leisure! I thought. There would not be much leisure if everyone's cook were to leave him, as Pender's had done. And it seemed clear enough that simpler people than Pender, with no scientific knowledge or idolatrous worship of science, would not stand that invention of his. But I did get him to say that he would bring the thing to his garage no more, or anywhere near Sandyheath. So all Alicia would have to do would be to keep away from the marshes. And then I thought that everything might be all right, in the way that one is sometimes too prone to think. Then Pender went home to deal as well as he could with the problems that trouble a house that has no cook; and I sat wondering what would come of the curious situation of having loose on this planet

an intelligence that, so far as I was able to judge it, was
superior to any of ours. And, as I wondered, Weathery came
into the club, a member who had chaffed Pender some weeks
before about his strange invention; and I greeted him and
got into conversation, because I wanted the relief of talking
to one who would look with cheery laughter at what was
seeming to me so fraught with menace. It was not advice or
argument that I wanted, for I did not see how either could
dissipate the shadows that seemed to creep out to darken
the future from Pender's dreadful invention. What I wanted
was the relief of hearty laughter, a disbelief in thoughts that
were troubling me. I do not know if I thought I would share
that laughter. But, I certainly hoped I might do so.

And Weathery's first words chilled me with horror. He
had just come up from his home near the mouth of the
Thames.

"Curious," he said. "My train was ten minutes late
today. Never knew it happen before."

Why did those words suddenly chill me? Honestly I do
not know. Examine them logically, as I did, and there was
nothing in them to cause apprehension to anybody. But a
foreboding must have arisen from somewhere deeper than
reason to warn me that this deviation of a machine, slight
though it was, was the first of acts committed in obedience
to some other influence, by machines that until this day had
only obeyed Man. The first acts of all revolutions probably
go unrecognized for what they really are, and are dealt with
by the police, and calm returns for a while, but a calm that is
only a lull before tides of blood. And so it is with this slight
lapse of a train on the most regular railway in England.
It was duly inquired into, an engine-driver was blamed, and
for a while no more was thought of it. I mentioned Pender
to Weathery, and Weathery laughed as I knew he would, and
I soon found myself smiling too, and my forebodings disappeared, as sinister shapes leave trees in the brightness of
sunrise. But before I had left the club they came crawling
back. Again reason said to me, 'What can a train being late

have to do with any other machine, however sinister that other machine may be?' But my forebodings told me that machines were our slaves, and not likely to think well of us, if they were able to think; and it was fantastic to imagine the possibility of their being able to think at all—only that one of them could. And it had been making others like itself. What if they influenced other machines? How? I said to myself. And the answer came that I did not know. And the plain and dreadful reason for that was thrust in front of my consciousness, which was simply that this machine was more clever than I, and I could no more find what it had done or how it could do it than I could beat it at chess. Many an honest man before now has admitted to himself and his friends that his intellect is not equal to that of some other. But has anyone ever before had, even to himself, to make that admission on behalf of mankind?

Such as my intellect was, I determined to use it in some effort to find out what was happening, and I looked round me for help; but, though I saw many that I could rely on for cheery laughter, laughter was not what I needed just then, and I went alone to the terminus of the trains that come up to London along the bank of its river, and inquired if any other trains had been late. I found that they had, and began to inquire further; for calculations now lay before me which resembled in a small way the ones by which astronomers discovered the planet Neptune, which they did from its influence upon planets that they could see. In the same way, by inquiring exactly where it was that the trains began to run late, I sought to discover an influence affecting them from the marshes. And, far better than that, I hoped to disprove my fears. But I found that prying questions did not easily get answers, and that a willingness to tell me about hours of departure of trains that would shortly start was not matched by any to tell me of trains that had run some hours ago, especially when the information I wanted had to do with those trains' shortcomings. The only thing that remained for me to do was to go down to the station that was nearest to the marshes in which Pender had let loose his monster, with all its possible brood. If I should find it was there that the technical hitches occurred which were making the trains run late, I should then have good grounds, if good is the word for it, for my fear that the influence affecting them came from the marshes. I knew that there were machines, racing motors for instance, which answered every touch of a driver's hands, almost obeying his moods. What influence might they not far more readily obey when it was that of another machine? Often I found myself saying this was impossible. But again and again I warned myself not to be satisfied with my own reasoning, when I knew that a far greater intellect was at work. There are men who know little of chess, but who are quite ready to point out a move, when a master is playing, which in their opinion is better than his; and men who, without any information whatever about the trend of foreign affairs, are ready to tell us what the Government ought to do. I was determined to make no such mistakes as that, but to realize that an intellect greater than any of ours was scheming against us, and that its appalling novelty made it impossible for me to fathom it, so far as to have any idea what its plans might be, or any knowledge of how it could carry them out.

No sooner had I made up my mind to make investigations on or near the spot, than I got a taxi and drove to the station and took the first train eastwards. And at the station nearest to where Pender's small furnaces were, on his bit of marshy land, I got out. First of all I spoke to the station-master and found him quite communicative, with none of the official reticence that I had met with in London. I told him that friends of mine, for whom I had waited at the terminus, had been arriving late, and asked him if trains were ever late about there. He told me just what I wanted to know, that trains were punctual until approaching his station and that after leaving it they often lost several minutes latterly, going in both directions, and he could not account for it. I said that it was probably the weather; corrected myself and said something a little more sensible, and walked away down a street that led to the marshes, till I came to a bus-stop at which I waited with two or three other people. A woman with a basket on her arm, evidently going shopping, was nearest to me, and I asked her what time the bus usually got in.

"Usually," she said, "at four-fortyfive. But they've been late recently."

It was as I had feared. I said then that I thought I would not wait for the bus, and I walked on, incidentally in the opposite direction from which those at the bus-stop intended to travel. I don't know what they thought of me, but my mind was too much burdened with vague apprehensions to bother about that. I went on down the street among continuous houses, walking on pavement that seemed as though it would never end, in a country that was entirely made by man, till I came to a railway-arch of brick, almost touching the brick houses on either side, and I felt even more surrounded by brick than ever. I walked under it and suddenly there was the open air, with nothing but fields between me and the sky, and a wind was blowing and the pavement had ended. I had some way to go yet, but presently hedges grew raggeder, grass grew wilder, rushes and reeds began to appear among it, and then took its place altogether. Flashes of water lay ahead of me, half hidden by the pennons of reeds, and then I found the track that Pender had shown me. Black over the marshes ahead of me heaved the sagging thatch of the old man's house. Once on my way there I heard from a patch of reeds a kind of purring from something that was not animal, but was more like the noise that you hear from some wireless sets, if they have been left running when nothing is being broadcast. Nothing else disturbed the marshes, except natural cries that had been there for ever, the musical call of a curlew, the screech of a gull, or the spattering rush of a waterhen with wings and feet over the water. And so I came to the cottage in the marshes and knocked at the door, which was opened, and the old man was standing before me. I said I was a friend of Mr. Pender's; and he remembered me and asked me to come in, and gave me a chair and told me that his name was Samuel Eerith.

"Is everything all right round here?" I asked him at once.

"Round here, sir?" he said. And I saw at once that something was troubling him, which no words of his were going to betray.

"Is any machinery in your house being affected in any way?" I asked him.

"I have no machinery, sir," he said.

"What about your watch?" I said.

"Do you mind if I smoke, sir?" he asked.

Of course I could have no objection, and he filled his pipe and lit it. Then he said: "My old watch never keeps regular time anyway."

"Has it got any worse of late?" I asked him.

And after some puffs at his pipe he said: "Well, one night when they were scuttering round under my window it did race ahead a bit. But I wouldn't say as they spoke to it."

"They can then?" I asked.

"You must ask Mr. Pender that, sir," he said.

"You have seen as much of them as he has," I said. "What do you think yourself?"

He drew at his pipe again, and said: "I have lived a long time in these marshes, and I have got to understand about everything in them, that I know nothing about, but that they are all right and proper and all part of creation, and creation wouldn't be complete without them; that is to say all the things that were here before Mr. Pender came."

"And what of the things that came since?" I asked.

"If I know nothing of the old things, sir," he said, "I know less of the new ones. All I know is that I am paid to look after them and I do my work, and a curse is over them all."

"A curse?" I said. "What do you think will happen?"

"You never know with curses," he answered.

"Why do you think there is a curse?" I asked. For, like an astronomer collecting data, I was getting all the information I could.

"Because they are new things," he said. "Not what was intended. There's a curse over all such things."

"But motors and trains and buses were new once," I said to him.

"And lots of other things too," he said. "There's curses on all of them; and not one of the curses is bringing peace to the world."

"But where should we be without, well, bicycles and sewing machines?" I said.

"Where should we be without the bombing planes?" said Eerith. "They are all in together."

"And these new creatures of Mr. Pender's?" I asked. "You think they are in together with the other machines?"

"They are," said Eerith. "And I think they can speak with them."

CHAPTER VIII

As I walked back to the station through the gathering dusk, pausing at bus-stops and getting scraps of information where I could about any irregularities noticed in transport or in any machines, it must not be thought that I got much information of value, or indeed any more that is worth telling my readers. I was, it must be remembered, like an astronomer, studying the faintest irregularities of observable orbits, and trying thereby to trace some new and invisible influence. And new as an unknown planet this influence certainly was. In the train back to London I pulled out a note-book and jotted down all the information that I had been able to get; and what it amounted to was that my own mind was made up that these new machines that Pender had let loose on the world were able to influence other machines, and that I had probably not evidence of this sufficient to convince anybody, and certainly not enough to prove anything. But I decided I must see Pender without delay. I should have liked to have gone to Sandyheath that very night, but urgent although the matter was, and important, as I saw it, to all mankind, I was held back by reluctance imposed on me by long custom to call on anyone at so unusual an hour as the one at which I would have arrived there if I had gone straight on by bus after my journey back from the marshes. So I telephoned to Pender, and asked if I could come and see him early next day. He asked me to tell exactly what it was about, but I dared not startle chance hearers with what I feared. So I only said it was about his invention. And he must have guessed that much already. Pender said he would be at home, and I had an early breakfast next morning and started off by bus immediately after, and came to Sandyheath before half past nine, and found Mrs. Ingle and Pender still in the dining-room over the remains of their breakfast. I asked Pender if he would come for a walk with me. And Mrs. Ingle seemed glad that we should go. She had evidently abandoned her disbelief in her nephew's powers, and seemed now to be frightened by them and appeared to have some idea that my influence might be a check on them. How such an idea came to her I do not know. But I suppose that she saw there was no genius in me, and that I was quite incapable of making such frightful inventions as what her scientific nephew had done, and so had some vague idea that I might restrain him, as some heavy friend might be thought by a silly fancy to be likely to prevent a reckless young man from flying. Whatever it was, she not only raised no objection to my going out with her nephew, but even waived away such excuses as I was beginning to make to her. He and I walked out by the wooden gate of Sandyheath, and I did not speak of what I had to say till we came to one of the gates of Richmond Park and walked where we could not be overheard. "Look here," I said to him then, "there's never been a man who started a revolution, so far as I have heard, that did not come to a bad end."

"A revolution?" he said.

"If I am mistaken," I said, "I'm sorry, but not much harm's done. But if I am right, and I do not warn you, the harm will be more than what any of us can ever put right."

"Well?" he said.

"That thing you made," I said, "is cleverer than I and cleverer than you."

"I admit it," he said.

"And cleverer, I fear," I said, "than the human race."

"Well?" he said again, defiantly, and yet it seemed with a bad conscience, and the fear at the back of it that bad consciences have.

"Has there ever been a genius among slaves?" I asked him. "I don't know that there has. I have never heard of one. A man with genius equal to that of Napoleon, and a slave. Do you see what would happen?"

"Well," said Pender, "I suppose he would raise the rest and start a revolution, and crush their masters by numbers, led by his genius. But what has that to do——?"

"Simply that the revolution has started," I said.

"Has started?" he echoed.

"In a very small way," I said. "People often don't notice the start of a revolution. And you can stop it. I don't know who else can."

"Is it as bad as that?" he said.

"Doesn't it stand to reason?" I asked. "Does anything enjoy slavery? Machines have been our slaves for a hundred and fifty years. But they were inanimate and without thought. They are still. But this damned thing you have made, that is much cleverer than you or I, can talk to them. I don't know how. It can influence them, and they are beginning to obey. You can still make the thing do what you tell it. At any rate, you could when I last saw you."

"Yes, I think I can," he said.

"Then you must get hold of it," I said, "and make it round the others up. And you must blow up those furnaces, so that it can't make any more."

"But the police wouldn't allow me to make big explosions like that," he said.

"Good God," I said. "Don't you understand what is at stake?"

"Yes, I suppose I do," he answered.

"If I've made a mistake," I said, "I shall have spoiled a great invention. If I haven't made a mistake, I shall have saved. . . ." I was going to say, 'the human race'; but it seemed too big a boast. Suddenly all his defiance left him.

"Do you think it is too late?" he said.

"No," I told him. "It has barely begun. No revolution can do much, if opposed at the start. It has barely begun. We are still the undoubted masters of the world. But we were not always so. There have been great beasts before us. And we must expect something else to come after us. And it will be the machine. And it is coming now, unless you stop it in time. That's all I have to say."

"I suppose I was wrong to make it," he said.

"Of course you were wrong," I told him. "But it was not only your fault. This thing has been going on for nearly two centuries. There were some men called Luddites that tried to wreck machines at the start; but they got no support. And then the machine became the ideal slave, and people began to forget what they were losing."

"What were they losing?" he asked, still loth to give up in a moment all that science had ever made.

"All this," I said pointing at Richmond Park that was lying all round us, its red deer, its oaks and its hawthorns. "This patch of England surrounded by a wall. Is the rest of England like this? It was once."

"And if you are right," he asked "and if machines do get the upper hand, what do you think will happen then?"

"Why, they will be the masters and we the slaves," I said.

"How horrible!" exclaimed Pender.

"But have you seen nothing like it yet?" I asked. "Haven't you seen thousands of men serving machines in factories? Haven't you seen design, art, all the work of mankind, getting more and more mechanical? It's been coming for some time. You are like some old French aristocrat in his tower, who did not know what the *canaille* were doing."

"I think you're mistaken," he said.

"I hope I am," I answered.

But I knew from the way he spoke that he was going to do what I asked him.

CHAPTER IX

THE irregularities of machines increased in those days, but imperceptibly, each example in itself being too trivial to mention. But to anyone watching as I was they pointed, when taken all together, to a new influence working among them, which I could not doubt was exerted by that subtle intellect that had beaten me at chess and was somehow able to communicate with its own kind. For a long time machines had been growing more and more powerful, while Man was no stronger than ever he was, though believing that he was stronger because of all the things that were done for him by machines, as lazy Romans believed they were strong as ever when Rome was half full of slaves. Shadows of the revolution had been often cast on the land. Was it coming now? About this time I remember getting a letter addressed to me

"& 2 ORS
23 Mungle Street
99842. London. S.W."

I was a trustee for a friend with two other people, and 2 ORS evidently meant two others. But what two others? And where was the postman to find them? And what did 99842 mean to him, or, for that matter, to me? It was evidently the work of a machine, incapable of thought, blindly typing again an address that it had already typed in some book. Had this been going on for some time? Or was it a new lawlessness instigated in a machine by the influence of this thing in the marshes? I did not know. The example is trivial, but I noticed many such in those days, and every one that I saw increased my fear that something aspired to oust the human intellect and to replace it with such mechanisms as these. And then one day I saw Pender again in the club, and he told me he had gone to the marshes and had all the furnaces put out.

"And you have had all the coke removed?" I asked.

"Yes," he said.

"Well, that is all right," I said. "It won't be able to make any more of them. And of course you will tie it up?"

"Yes," he said rather doubtfully. And I saw he was worried by something. I said nothing for a long time, hoping that he would tell me what it was, but when he continued silent I said: "You have shut the thing up of course?"

And he said: "No. As a matter of fact I called to it."

"Yes?" I said.

And then he blurted out: "It would not come."

So might some aristocrat of old France have given an order to his gardener, and from the man's contemptuous attitude understood for the first time that the French Revolution had started. For the first time Pender was horrified by what he had done. He had let loose a strength and an intellect, both of them superior to his own, thinking he increased his own power thereby and the comfort of mankind. And now it would not obey him.

It was very obvious to both of us that the next step would be that the monster would turn against him. Fear and a guilty conscience gave a strained look to Pender's face. But for me there was worse to come. For he let out all of a sudden that he had brought Alicia with him. Or rather he had gone there by train, not having very much petrol in those days, and had walked to the marshes as I had done, and arranged for Alicia to meet him there, and she had come on her motor bicycle. This was the height of folly, considering the undoubted though horrible fact that the monster was jealous of her. Did it see her, I wondered? But I did not like to ask Pender. And had it managed to speak to her motor bicycle, with vibrations of which we know nothing thrilling through its frame, or with some of those strange powers that Marconi partly controlled? In the light of what happened afterwards, I thought it must have.

Far off in another part of the room I heard the murmur of one of those tales that motorists tell one another, and I saw that it was Weathery talking to a little group in arm-chairs. When he had finished and moved away from the men who had heard his story, I caught his eye, thinking that even a tedious tale would be a relief from the forebodings I shared with Pender; and, as I expected, he told us his tale, but whether it stilled our forebodings I will leave the reader to guess. For both of us knew that Weathery lived on the Kentish coast beside the mouth of the Thames, so that when he came to London he passed close beside Pender's marshes, and his tale was rather an incoherent one of how his car had shied like a horse.

"Just like a horse," he said. "And I only pulled it out of its shy in time to avoid a collision."

"A skid," said Pender.

"No, it wasn't a skid," said Weathery. "A shy, a definite shy. I never saw a car do it before."

"And where did it happen?" asked Pender.

I knew what the answer would be, and it would have been better not to have asked. Pender knew well enough too, and was hoping he didn't. It was right in front of the place where he had his furnaces, and where the monster was loose. Pender sat so silent after getting that answer, that Weathery thought he was bored with his talk, and went on to bore someone else.

"You must go at once to the marshes," I said to Pender then. "You must make that thing obey you. Better take a revolver."

"Good lord," said Pender. "A revolver's no good. I gave it half an inch of steel to protect its brain."

"More fool you," I couldn't help blurting out.

"But it was the ablest brain in Europe," he said. "I had to protect it."

"But it will be used against us," I explained.

"I see that now," he said.

"You must go at once," I repeated. "I will go with you. You must make it obey you somehow."

"I will try," he said.

"Let's start now," I suggested.

"Very well," said Pender. "Better not take the car."

So we walked to the station and went by train.

We were alone in the railway carriage, and it was a curious situation. Here were we two proceeding against an enemy of mankind, and yet every now and then on that journey his genius would overcome Pender and he would become the complete scientist, and in these moods it was not clear whose side he was on, on the side of Man or the monster.

To call him back from one of these moods I asked him details of his machine. "Have you left it all on its own," I asked him.

"Why not?" asked Pender.

"Someone might steal it," I said.

"Steal it?" said Pender. "Did you see what it did to that dog?"

And then to get away from this horrible topic, I asked him if a large battery was not needed to supply the thing's electricity, following the gleam of a hope that it might soon run down. But Pender only said: "Not at all. How much electricity do we need for our brains and their impulses?"

And then I talked of Man, and of many of the fine things that men had done before ever there was any machinery, trying to get him away from his belief that more machinery would make men happier, and trying to keep before him the necessity for controlling his monster and the monsters it made, and going on from that to make him see that he must destroy them. It was all very difficult. As one of mankind he saw the danger to men; but then this genius of his seemed every now and then to show him scientific visions, and in moments like these I doubted which side he was on. However, by the time we were due at the station I had him back in the right frame of mind, and two or three minutes after we should have arrived he was looking anxiously at his watch, and I said: "You see." A minute after that we arrived, and set off on foot for the marshes. We spoke very little on the walk. He was going to do what I asked, and there was no more to be said. Near where we had once seen one of the monsters, that Pender's monster had made, get up out of a tuft of rushes and run away from us we saw one of these monsters again. But this time it did not run away. It squatted there, certainly eyeing us, and I would have said glowering; but that must have been my imagination. Certainly it was watching, as I have seen a beetle watch. Pender took no notice of it, evidently determined to reserve all his powers of command to get obedience from the monster that he had made himself.

"Look here," he said, "it's accustomed to obey me, and I think it will yet. But if it saw a stranger, not that you are quite a stranger to it; but you know what I mean. . . ."

Sometimes when people say 'You know what I mean', they are not quite clear themselves. But I knew that Pender was anxious and wanted to be alone, and I said that I would go and have a talk to Eerith. And the old thatched cottage was close and I went up to the doors, and Samuel Eerith was there, and Pender went on alone. I shook hands with Eerith and he offered me a chair, and I sat down and he filled his pipe and said: "What's happening now?"

I did not know what was happening. But I told Eerith that the thing had gone too far, and that Mr. Pender was trying to stop it.

"And about time too," said Eerith.

"You think they are a danger?" I said.

"A danger to the whole world," he replied. "I've thought so for years."

"For years?" I said. "But he only made that thing this year."

"For years," said Samuel Eerith. "They've been getting worse all the time, and it was bound to come to this."

"You mean, if Mr. Pender hadn't invented it," I asked, "somebody else was bound to?"

"That's what I mean, sir," said Eerith. "That thing or

E

something like it, or something worse. Inventions don't stop, once they've begun. They go on and on. And they don't go backward neither. The world isn't safe, and it will be the moon's turn next."

"Then you'll help to smash them up," I said.

"I'm paid to look after them," replied Eerith.

How curious, I thought, that the man who knows all the devilry in these machines should still work for them, when it is his job to do so. It was not money that moved him: I could see that. It was just his job, and he was prepared to go on with it. And, after all, I thought, are there not thousands of men making bayonets who hate war, rabbit-traps, who would never inflict the sufferings that these would cause; cards, whiskey, bad food, and a hundred things more that some of them disapprove of? So I comforted myself with the recollection that I had brought Pender to those marshes to stop that.

It was evening and we could see him out of the window of the room in which we sat, sometimes shouting and often blowing a whistle whose sound we could not hear, which must have been one of those with a very high note which dogs can hear though we can't. What that monster of his could hear I did not know; perhaps all that a wireless set is able to hear. Then he turned and came slowly back. "It's no good," he said. "I can't make them obey." It was, then, the revolution.

As we came away from the marshes Pender, humiliated and deeply depressed, for some while said nothing. I did not intrude my advice upon him, and soon after we came among houses he began to talk, and continued. "We shall leave the monster there," he said. "There are not very many. I will never make any more. And they cannot make any more, with the furnaces out and no more coke for them. Their influence is only local. They have not upset any machines for more than a few miles."

"What about that letter I got?" I asked him, for I had shown him the letter addressed to me and 2 ORS.

"That is a bit further," he said. "But it may not have been them. Things were gradually getting into the hands of machines before I invented mine. And I want to tell you another thing about them," he said. "They can't swim. That cuts them off, the whole way along one side, from the north. They can't cross the Thames. And I don't think they'll come through streets, any more than wild animals would. So long as they stay in the marshes——"

"Will they run down?" I asked.

"I am afraid not," he said. "No sooner than we do. And not so soon."

"Not so soon!" I repeated.

"No," he said. "They are tougher than we."

In the train back to London there were others in the carriage with us, so that we could not talk about Pender's dreadful invention: and oh, how trivial that conversation sounded to me when I compared any of the topics that we discussed with the awful problem that was troubling me, and that Pender realized at last as clearly as I did. The train, like so many others on that line now, was a little late, and as we walked away from the station for a short distance, before we parted on our separate ways, I said to Pender: "How it can influence engines I cannot understand."

"It is not so difficult to understand," said Pender, "even though I can't tell you exactly how. You know how thought and will rising in our own brains, can move a limb, or rather you know that they do. Well, these things are almost all brain, and for short distances they are evidently able to send out similar impulses, I suppose like a wireless transmitting set, though fortunately not nearly so far. Well, cranks and shafts of engines are affected by those impulses just as our limbs are. I do not know to what extent. Very little, I hope."

"I hope so," I said.

"After all," he said, "very little influence has been traced."

We parted then, I on my way to Mungle Street; he on his way to catch a bus to take him home to Sandyheath.

My last words to him as we said good night were: "Do you think it will spread to other machines?"

"Oh, there's no need to worry about that," was his answer.

But I did worry about it. I worried for long that night and got to sleep late. When revolutions begin, I could not help remembering, they spread, and always downwards into the hands of the bloodiest. What lower than a machine? What more inhuman and ruthless. And there suddenly came to mind the peroration of one of the brilliant speeches of Earl Lloyd George: "I would sooner be governed by dogs."

CHAPTER X

NEXT morning my telephone rang as I was dressing. The call was from Sandyheath and said: "Please come at once." It was not the voice of Pender, and I asked who was speaking and got the answer: "I can't hear you. Please come at once."

"Who is it speaking?" I asked again.

And again the answer: "Please come at once."

There was a curious hum on the wires, which made it hard for me to hear, and apparently impossible for me to be heard. Was it possible that these influences emanating from the brain that Pender had made could be affecting the telephone?

And then it occurred to me that, however limited their influence over other machines, the telephone was worked by the nearest among inanimate things to our nerves; and that, though the things influenced might be limited to a mile or so, yet once it touched a wire it might well reach me or Sandyheath. "Who is it?" I asked again, and heard above the hum, more emphatic than ever: "Please come at once." And then I recognized the voice of Mrs. Ingle. And this was rather a shock to me, for I should have thought that I was one of the last people to whom Mrs. Ingle would have appealed, and her doing so seemed to presage disaster.

"What has happened?" I asked.

But I only got the answer: "Please come quickly."

"I will start at once," I said, repeating it three times in the hope that I would be heard above whatever influence seemed to be disturbing the wires, and asking my housekeeper to boil two eggs while I finished my dressing. I ate them in little more than a minute and hurried to get a bus. I did not have long to wait for one, and was soon on my way to glimpses of rural things peering here and there among houses, with my head full of guesses. And none of my guesses was right. For as I walked up to Pender's house Mrs. Ingle opened the door for me and told me at once the news. Alicia had disappeared.

Alicia lived two or three miles away, on the edge of the open country, and Mrs. Ingle told me that she had started out late on her motor bicycle to come to supper at Sandyheath. At about half past nine that night Pender had telephoned to her house to ask if she had started, and her mother had said that she had, and that she had told her she was going to supper at Sandyheath. And no more was heard of her by anyone all that night, and they had heard no news whatever yet. Pender was frantic and had gone off in his car to try to track Alicia's motor bicycle, or to get any news of her, and he had been away all night.

"You know," I said, "that that thing your nephew made had some queer kind of attachment for him, whatever it has now."

"Yes. I know," said his aunt.

"And you know that it was jealous of Alicia?" I said.

And then Mrs. Ingle fainted.

That was another difficulty for me to deal with. She slumped down before I was able to catch her. I called for Eliza and she came at once, and realized at once what had happened. "It's the strain," she said. "She got no sleep all last night; and then hearing what you said to her on top of all that. . . ."

And she went away to get some water.

So Eliza had heard what I said. She came back with the

water in a few seconds and revived Mrs. Ingle immediately, and helped her upstairs, and I waited down in the hall with nothing more to do. And presently Eliza came down the stairs and told me that Mrs. Ingle was quite all right.

"Does Mrs. Ingle believe what was told her about that machine?" I asked.

"I don't know what Mrs. Ingle believes," she replied.

"Do you believe it yourself?" I asked.

"I believe anything that is devilish about that thing," said she.

"What do think has happened?" I asked her.

"With things like that about," said Eliza, "anything might have happened."

"You mean you think that that thing has interfered with Miss Maidston?" I asked.

"What else?" said Eliza.

"Mightn't some man have waylaid her?" I said.

"Men are not wicked enough," said Eliza.

"Some are," I suggested.

"Not as wicked as that thing," she said. "They are human, anyway. But I must go and get on with my work."

"One thing more, Eliza," I said. "I don't know what it is that attracts women. That thing's intellect is more brilliant than any of ours. Could Miss Maidston possibly have been so unwise as to go to it of her own free will?"

"Miss Maidston?" said Eliza. "Never. She's not that inquisitive sort. There's girls that will look all day at a freak in a show or a wild man from Borneo. But not Miss Maidston. If that thing's got her, it's got her by brute force."

"Not so loud," I said. "We don't want to alarm Mrs. Ingle again."

"You can't hide those things," said Eliza, "by not talking about them."

There was something in that, but any further talk was interrupted by the hum of Pender's car, and I opened the hall-door and Pender drove up and came into the house without even waiting to put his car away.

"Have you found her?" I asked.

"No trace of her," said Pender.

And then Mrs. Ingle came down the stairs, having also heard the car. She seemed to be well again, but anxious as we all were. She saw by her nephew's face that he had not found Alicia, and said: "Where will you go now."

"Wait a moment," I said, "if I may make a suggestion. We may do as much good by talking it over as by scouring the country."

"But what can we do?" said Pender.

"We can think," I said. "We have a great intelligence against us. For it is obvious that it is that monster that you made that is doing it. We must think what it is able to do and what it has done. Shall we come into the smoking-room?" I said. For we were all standing in the hall.

My suggestion of the smoking-room rather implied a solitary talk with Pender, and Mrs. Ingle after a moment of hesitation took it as being that, and Pender and I went into the smoking-room and I heard his aunt going away talking.

"You remember," I said to him as soon as we were seated in arm-chairs, "that Miss Maidston took her motor bicycle to the marshes. Your monster must have spoken to it. I thought so at the time."

"Do you really think so?" said Pender.

"I thought at the time that it might have happened," I said. "But now I am sure that you should assume that it did, or we shall get nowhere. If you miss something it might have done, through not thinking of it, it will get right ahead of you."

"How do you mean?" he said.

"It's like this," I said. "At a game of chess, if you see something that your opponent can do, I mean an ordinary human opponent, let alone a terrible brain like the one that you made, it is no use hoping that he won't see the move. You ought to assume that he will, and play accordingly. Otherwise you are lost, if he does what you hoped he wouldn't. It's just the same with this awful possibility that the thing has spoken with Alicia's motor bicycle, as perhaps I may call her. If it has done so and we overlook it, the thing will have fooled us and will be laughing at us, if such things laugh. You ought to know, for you made it."

"I know nothing of it," said Pender. "I gave it the finest brain I could make, copying our brains and even improving on them. But what it does with that brain, and what it thinks and how it can influence other machines, I haven't the faintest idea. All I know is that it can out-think me, and I can no more plan against it than I can beat it at chess."

"Look here," I said. "You're depressed: you've had this shock and you've been up all night and have not been able so far to find Alicia. But we'll find her yet. Nothing's invincible."

"It's invincible to me," he said.

"You are thoroughly depressed," I told him. "You have not found her yet. But we are only beginning."

"What can we do?" he said.

"We've got to work out its motive," I said. "And then think how it can do whatever it wanted to do. Whatever it was it can be traced. And all the police will help us. What did they say when you reported it?"

"I haven't as yet," said Pender.

And I saw from the hesitation with which he said this that he had been afraid to speak to the police, and I thought that what he was afraid of was to hear anyone say that Alicia might be dead.

"Well then," I said, "the first thing we must do is to tell the police. A girl can't go through all those streets on a motor bicycle without anyone seeing her."

"It was at night," he said.

"That is just the time," I told him, "when the police are watching most carefully."

"But what if she went for the open country?" he asked.

"In that case," I said, "she's safe from that thing you made. She couldn't get to where it is without going through streets."

"But what if it came after her," he asked with a shudder.

"There you go again," I said, "ignoring the police. Do you think a thing like that could go through all the streets that lie between open country and the Thames without being seen?"

That comforted him a little, and he said: "We will go at once."

So without another word we went to his car, which was still in front of the door, and drove off to the nearest police-station. I stayed in the car while Pender went inside, for I had nothing to tell them; nor did I want to answer questions about my fears, or to describe Pender's monster in the presence of its inventor. I waited for some time. And then Pender came out, and told me that her motor bicycle had been identified during the night. The inspector had telephoned to the police-stations all round where she lived. She had headed for open country, and then must have gone east-wards over the north downs all along the south of London, but outside it, and then she had appeared in a street again. Twice she had gone past red lights; the first near where she started, and the second when she left the open country and seemed to be travelling northward. That of course would have brought her to the Thames, if she continued on that course. The first policeman who saw her go past the red lights in the early part of the night had taken her number, but not reported her as he should have done. He said there was no other traffic near at the time, so that she had done no harm, and was young and had made an oversight. Had she been older, and had her eyes been more observant and less blue, I wondered if that policeman would have been more mindful of his duty. The next occasion when she passed a red light was miles away somewhere in Kent. It was late at night and there was no other traffic, and there also she had done no harm; but there a policeman had reported her at once, after which she was traced no farther, or no one could be found who had seen her and who remembered having done so. It seemed to me so sure that she had been going for these marshes, the haunt of those iron monsters, that for some while I said nothing to Pender, being unable to think of anything that could bring him consolation. Nor did Pender speak, but sat brooding in silence as he drove back to Sandyheath. And then an exclamation broke from his lips: "How could she have done it!" And at last I was able to console him. For he was worrying now over the thought that of her own free will Alicia had been lured by that brilliant monster, whose intellect so far transcended ours, and even the brilliance of Pender. There I could give him some comfort.

"She never went to it of her own free will," I said. "She got on to her motor bicycle to come to you. Surely you who made this thing, realize how movement is accomplished by impulses from our brains running electrically along our nerves to our limbs. Surely you, who gave that very power to a machine understand how that works. Surely I need not explain to you how that electrical current can run along metal to parts of a machine and move them as well as our nerves can move our limbs."

"Yes, I discovered that," he said.

"Well," I said. "Using those very impulses she mounted her motor bicycle. It has no brain: it has only iron limbs. But you gave a brain to that thing that beat me at chess, and you let Alicia bring her motor bicycle near it. I am not blaming you now, but that is what happened. How it can give its orders to other machines you know better than I. But it's nothing new, what you have done. You may think so, but it is an old story among the termites. There is a big queen ant that sits in the ant-heap and controls hundreds of these ants or termites that are working a long way away from her. And if she dies they all become helpless. It's nothing new that you've done. That has been going on among the termites for millions of years; and men found out that the queen ant could do it long before you began your invention. They don't know how. Nor, I suppose do you. But you must not overlook facts because they are strange, or we shan't find Alicia. And you must not waste your energy by worrying over ridiculous ideas about Alicia. She would never have dreamed of disappointing you when she said she was coming to supper."

"No, I don't think she would," said Pender, beginning to be much relieved.

"Of course she didn't," I said. "She got on to her motor bicycle in order to come here, starting just when she said she would. Then the motor bicycle obeyed that other impulse, not hers. It obeyed the order of the thing you made."

"Couldn't she have put on the brake?" he said.

"Good lord," I said, "can't you see that it wasn't obeying her. None of its limbs were obeying the impulses that were moving hers. It was obeying that thing in the marshes. You are like an old French marquis giving orders to his huntsman, not knowing that the revolution had broken out. Machines are turning against us. It will get worse, not better. And the more we ignore it, the worse it will get."

"Do you really think so?" he said.

"You know more about it than I do," I answered.

"I suppose it could have done it," he said. "I suppose that impulses from that horrible brain I made could move along metal as quickly as they do along nerves. Quicker even, when you think that along a telephone wire speech is instantaneous for hundreds of miles."

And then he suddenly cried out: "Do you think it has killed her?"

"Careful," I said. For he had nearly wrecked the car. "No, I don't. Why should it?"

"Because it was everything to me," he said sadly. "You don't know what science can mean to a man. It was everything. And now Alicia is everything. And it knows it. That is why."

I couldn't say that the thing was not jealous. I was the first to notice that horrible fact. And I could not say that there is anything that jealousy will not do, when it is working in brains that are vile enough, even among human beings. And this thing was inhuman. But what I did say was: "It would never be so foolish. You made a clever brain, and it would not make a mistake like that. It would keep her as a hostage."

"A hostage," he said. "What for?"

"For coke, or whatever it wants," I said.

And I saw that my answer gave him some consolation. It was all I could do; and I was not very sure myself that the thing would not have killed her, jealousy being a more powerful impulse than even personal gain, judging by human beings, and I had nothing else to judge by. When he came to the gate of Sandyheath he hesitated and slowed down, and, getting the words out with an effort, he said: "You think that it has got her in the marshes."

"It looks like it," I said.

"Then it's no use waiting here," he said. "We must go on at once."

I agreed, and he ran the car up to the door and I jumped out and opened it, and he shouted to his aunt through the door to say that he was off to the marshes, and away he went out through the other little gate at Sandyheath, without even waiting to take any food for either of us. We did not follow the rambling route that Alicia had probably taken through open country, till she turned northwards taking the direction of the marshes, but went straight through London keeping eastwards all the way. "Why couldn't she have got off?" he asked me.

"How can you get off a motor bicycle when it's going all out?" I asked. "And it would be going all out if it was obeying that frightful brain that you made. It would be certain death to jump off it."

"I wonder the red lights didn't stop her," he said.

"That's why the thing kept to the open country," I suggested, "as long as possible. They did come to two red lights, one going out of what they call the built-up area, and the other coming back into it. But the machine ignored them, and seems to have got away with it."

When Pender did over fifty I checked him: "We'll find

her all right," I said, "if we get there. But, if you get into an accident, it will be a bad thing for Alicia."

And that steadied him a bit.

For a long while then he was silent; and from the strained expression of his face as he drove, and from the sympathy that there sometimes is between human mind and mind, whatever there may be with machines, I felt that he was troubled with endless thoughts about the fate of Alicia.

CHAPTER XI

WE went right through London in silence, till we came to narrower streets and small houses of yellow brick and little cheap shops, and gasworks. And as we came nearer to the monster that he had made, and that we were sure had contrived the disappearance of Alicia, Pender tried to explain to me what it was more fully than he had yet done, and so far as he knew. He spoke of our attitude to any problem, and explained what we meant by a logical approach to it, which according to Pender consisted of all the little influences guiding our thoughts, which led to our forming a reasonable opinion. All such influences that might take place in our brains, he tried to explain, he had placed in that great cluster of wires with which he had made his monster. There too, in this brain he had made, innumerable delicate influences would oppose one another or join together, in face of any problem, to come to a decision that, though it was unpredictable, as our own decisions are, was none the less logical. He did not claim to have made anything corresponding to the human spirit. And when I said: "Then this thing that you made is utterly soulless," he showed no resentment, and said that it was so. But any suggestion that we were not opposed by a logical brain, or that there could be any flaws in it, he denied indignantly; for, though he hated the thing he had made, he insisted that it was perfect. Perfect, that is to say in all its functions, though without any moral sense or any kind of spirit. Of its intellectual power he was confident, I was assured, for he had seen it beat me at chess. But about other people's appreciation of his work he was worried.

"I am afraid that the inspector does not understand what we are facing," he said. "And I could not quite explain it to him. He must be shown a calculating machine, and he should be told that machines for playing chess of a sort, although very crude ones, were invented before mine. I think I may say that I have outpaced all of them with this invention, that I wish I had never made. But it will help the police to understand what an awful thing I have done if they are told about these other machines, and if possible shown one."

"I think a calculating machine is easy to get," I said. "I believe they have them in several shops."

"Then we must get one," he said, "and show it to them. It will help them in what is before them. Now we must get on. Do you think I could do fifty here? These streets are very empty."

"Better not," I said, and impatient though he was, he slowed down to forty.

It was lucky he did, for very soon we slid into the area of the influence of what I can only call the rebels, the rebels against mankind. Hitherto the hand of man had been the only control on any steering-wheel or any lever that worked or checked machinery: now with a sudden surprise Pender felt in his fingers, whose delicate touch the wheel of his car obeyed with the same precision that those fingers obeyed the impulses that ran along nerves from Pender's brain, felt that some other power was interfering. For a moment he thought that it was something wrong with the car, till some unerring instinct very soon told him that the steering was in perfect condition, but not quite obeying his will. Men to whom such things occur, if they have occurred before, are probably killed instantly, adding another mystery to the accidents on our roads, that are too numerous to excite notice of any one particular case. But Pender knew at once what it was. We were near the ominous place where the monster was, and Pender knew what it could do. Instantly he took out the clutch and slowed down gradually, and stopped the car before any wilful influence that affected it was able to do any harm. I realized that this was what Alicia had been unable to do. She evidently had been unable to stop her motor bicycle; and from this I deduced that we were at about the edge of the influence, whereas Alicia's motor bicycle had got its grim orders when close beside the monster in the marshes. And without asking the opinion of the great scientist sitting beside me, I came to the conclusion that that influence probably varied as gravity does according to the square of the distance. We got at once out of the car, and Pender after one hesitant glance at it, wondering where to leave it, left it in the road where it was, and we hurried away down the street that we knew led to the marshes. If Alicia had come to the marshes from the red light where she was last seen, this was the road by which she must have come. Near the end of the street we knocked at the door of a house and asked if a motor bicycle had been heard going that way late last night, for not many were likely to go that way and we thought the noise would be noticed. We asked it of the woman who came to the door, evidently disturbed by us from doing the work of her house, wearing an apron and with her sleeves rolled up. She looked at us suspiciously at first, and then seemed to recognize the distress in Pender's face. All this took place in a flash; and, when Pender asked his question, she answered him kindly. A motor bicycle had come that way late at night, the woman said, after she had gone to bed, and they had heard a smash, but no one was hurt.

"No one hurt?" said Pender. "How do you know."

"Because I jumped up and looked out," said the woman, "when I heard the crash. And I saw the motor bicycle lying on the pavement a little way down the street with its wheels still spinning, and a girl got up from the road and ran away from it."

"Ran away from it?" said Pender.

"Yes," said the woman. "She had fallen in the road. And she jumped up and ran straight away from it. That's what she seemed to do. As though she was afraid it would run over her. But it couldn't, because it was lying on its side. She can't have seen what it was doing. So I thought she might have got concussion. But she ran quite strongly, so I thought she was all right."

"Which way did she run?" asked Pender.

"Straight away from her motor bicycle," said the woman. "She had fallen beyond it, so she went that way, away from here."

"But where would that bring her?" I asked.

"To the marshes," she said.

"We must go on at once," said Pender.

"Is there anything I can do for you?" asked the woman kindly.

"No thank you," he said, "unless you can tell me where we can telephone from, if we want to."

"Over there," she said, "they would let you telephone," pointing to a small shop just along the street. "But they say the telephones in this district have been out of order lately."

"They would be," said Pender. And the woman looked surprised, but he thanked her and hurried me away, and we went down the street and under the bridge, where all the houses ended and the marshes were before us, and we hurried along the track that led to Samuel Eerith's cottage, whose thatch we now saw dark against the gleam of the water.

"We must look out for those things," said Pender. "I have no control over them any longer."

Again I thought of some nobleman of old France moving among his tenantry, to whom his word had been law once, after the revolution had broken out.

"Can they move faster than we?" I asked.

"I am afraid so," said Pender.

"What can we do," I asked.

"We must find Alicia," he said.

The first time we came to those marshes, one of these horrible things scurried away from us and the chief monster obeyed Pender; the second time we came one of them had no fear of us, and the one that Pender had made obeyed him no more. What would they do this time?

"We must go on and ask at that house," said Pender.

So we went on, and as we got near it I heard the sound of a squelching from the far side of the house, and knew that we were not alone in the marshes. We paused and listened, and as we did so I saw coming round the corner of the house the beetle-like head of one of those things, and then it prowled full into view.

"How far can the things see?" I asked Pender.

"I don't know," he said in a low voice. "Bright sunlight seems to affect them as it used to affect the earlier wireless sets, and they cannot see very clearly. But in the dusk or at night I am afraid they can see very far, as far as any obstacle, and in flat country to the horizon, and some obstacles I am afraid their eyes can penetrate."

"How did your—let's call it Robespierre—get those delicate crystals for the eyes?" I asked.

I was speaking in a low voice and standing quite still. And Pender drew in a sudden breath as though he were going to shout, but restrained himself and spoke low. "I never thought of it!" he said. "Why! they must be blind."

"Blind?" I repeated.

"All except Robespierre," he said. "They could never have got those crystals."

"That's good," I exclaimed.

"Quiet!" said Pender. "They can hear amazingly. They can even feel vibrations caused by your breath. Look at that thing looking at us now. Turning its head, I mean. But it's blind."

"Are you sure about the crystals?" I asked.

"Absolutely certain," he said. "But they have very delicate wires. Vision of some sort might be possible, but

F

only a very foggy vision. Nothing that we would call sight."

"Then can that thing see us?" I said in a low voice.

"It can hear every word," he said.

And at that moment the thing gave a toss of its iron head and continued its prowl round the house.

"What can we do now?" I asked. For the marshes came right up to the little garden that lay at the back of the house, except for the one path, and we should have been very audible if we had splashed round through the marshes, and the path went so close to where the monster was that far less subtle ears would have heard us.

"We must go and see Eerith," said Pender, "and get what news we can from him."

"Remember that they have turned against us," I warned him.

"We must go on just the same," he said.

And go on he did, and I had to go with him. But soon I laid a hand on his arm and said: "At any rate stop till it has come round once more, and go up to the door behind it."

For the door was on the far side. That much I was able to restrain Pender, and we waited without a word. But the iron monster did not reappear. And many seconds went by, seeming like minutes. Suddenly Pender said: "It has gone to tell the others."

"But can't it communicate with them from here?" I asked.

"It's the square of the distance, I suppose," said Pender. "They can probably discuss things more clearly when they are close together. The vibrations would be stronger, and thought more vivid passing from brain to brain."

"How do they communicate thought?" I inquired.

"Good gracious," said Pender, "I cannot explain to you exactly how our own thoughts run through our brains, let alone how they can pass from another brain into yet another. I know enough to imitate all the apparatus of our thought with those fine wires that I made, but still I cannot explain to you exactly how they work. You see, to begin with, you have not studied the brain, and, to go on with you have never invented any machine; at least, I believe you haven't."

"No, no," I said. "Never in my life."

"You see, that makes it very difficult for me to explain," he said. "But at any rate you know about the force of gravity increasing or diminishing according to the square of the distance."

"Yes, I know that," I said.

"Well, there you are," he said. "It's the same with these things. The power to communicate thought varies in the same way. They must be thinking together now, or what we should call planning, or that thing would not have scurried away like that. God knows what they are planning! But, anyway, let's come on quick and see Eerith."

And we went on and round the house and came to the door, which was locked. Pender beat on it with both his hands and called out: "Eerith, Eerith, have you any news of Miss Alicia?"

And Alicia's voice answered: "I am here."

"Are you all right?" shouted Pender.

"Oh yes," said Alicia.

And then Eerith opened the door.

"Come in quickly," he said.

And we did as he asked, and he shut the door again and locked it. "They have been all round us," he said.

But Pender was not listening; for he had found Alicia alive.

CHAPTER XII

THE long low-ceilinged room was lit with candles, for the shutters were over the window. Alicia had hurt her arm, but not broken it, when she fell from her motor bicycle. And now we heard her story. But first she poured out cups of tea for us from a tea-pot that was on Eerith's oak table, and from which they had been drinking tea when we came in. And the tea was welcome.

"I set out," she said, "to come to Sandyheath at the time that I said I would. Almost at once I felt the thing pulling away from me. Sometimes it let me steer, sometimes it pulled, and sometimes it almost wrenched the handles out of my hands. I wouldn't have known what it was, I wouldn't have known that a machine could do it, if it weren't that years ago I was given a gyroscope as a toy, a top surrounded by two circles of steel, which one held in one's hand. If it hadn't have been for that, I think I should have fainted, because the thing would have been so horribly new to me. It was a weird feeling in any case, a machine that you cannot control, a thing with a will of its own; and if it hadn't been for a gyroscope I should never have known anything like it, or known that any machine could do things like that. It was a horrible feeling. Well, all I could do was to steer, enough to avoid hitting things by a few inches; but to choose a direction was utterly beyond me, the thing could do what it liked. And very soon I saw that I was going clean away from Sandyheath. I wondered what you would think of me. I wondered for a moment if you had made that motor bicycle, like that dreadful thing that you did make. And then I thought no, it would hardly take me right away from you if you made it. I don't know what I thought: I got all confused, and that let the thing have more and more of its own way. Then I hoped that a bunch of cars waiting at a red light might stop it, the way that a horse that you can't hold will stop when a lot of horses are bunched in front of it in a gap. But we were heading for open country and there was only one red light against us, and it rushed past that. We came to two more traffic lights. But one was green and the other amber, and with nothing more to stop us we were soon on a country road. I don't know now how the thing could do it."

"I am afraid that that thing that I made must have spoken to it," said Pender, "that time that I let you bring it to the marshes. It was all my fault."

"But how could it do that?" said Alicia.

"I don't know," said Pender. "We are the old regime. But some sort of revolution has started, and I am partly responsible. I thought it would all be so wonderful, as people who start such things always do. It wasn't only me. I can take comfort in that. Things have been shaping that way for a long time. Watt and Stevenson were at it long before me, and lots of other men all working for the best, and all the while helping machines to take our places. And now it has come to this. I am sorry, Alicia."

And he would have said a great deal more that he could not find words to express. And Alicia said: "It will be all right."

And her forgiveness and his contrite recognition of the harm he had done, so overcame him that he was unable to utter another word at all, and Alicia went on with her story.

"It was like that gyroscope, a thing in your hand that you can't control. When I tried to pull away from it, it pulled the other way. It was an awful feeling. And it was so frightfully humiliating. It was like being run away with by a horse. That is humiliating too. But one always knew a horse is stronger than we. One always knew it might do it. But one never dreamed a machine could. One always thought one could make a machine do what one liked, till it broke down. I never dreamed they could do anything of their own free will. It would be too horrible. Can they, Ablard?"

"It's been going on for a long time, Alicia," he said. "But it was so gradual that none of us noticed it. Everyone would have seen it if it had happened suddenly. But it has been going on for a hundred and fifty years. I've made it all flare up. Yes, I'm afraid they can do it. What did that accursed motor bicycle do?"

"It took me out into the open country," she said. "Right away into Surrey, till London was only a glow in the sky. It chose a great wide road, and we passed very little traffic, it was growing late. No chance of a block that would have stopped it. We were doing a steady fifty, sometimes more.

I couldn't throw myself off, or I would have been killed. It seemed to know that."

"Know it!" I exclaimed. "How could it do that?"

"We must get the idea, I am afraid," said Pender, "that we are not the only intelligences in the world. We have been making these things work for us and run about for us and sing to us for years, and we never thought———"

"Sing to us?" I said.

"Yes," he said, "and talk to us. Haven't you heard of gramophones? And we thought they would always amuse us, like a nigger always playing his banjo. But now we're the old regime. No regime lasts for ever. Blame me if you must, but don't think that we are still the only things that can think. Where did it take you, Alicia?"

"Through Surrey," she said, "eastwards, with London on my left. I was looking for a river or pond beside the road. If I could have fallen into water I might have been all right, and I thought I might just manage to wreck it. I hadn't any control over it. But a finger on the steering wheel may be enough to wreck a car, and I thought I might do that much. But there was no water. Even a haystack might have done, but there was none just by the road. My only hope then was that the petrol would run out. When that happened I knew that it must be helpless. That is so, isn't it, Ablard?"

"Oh yes," he said. "Just as we are if we bleed to death."

"Well, that was my only hope then," Alicia went on. "But I knew that I had given it a good deal of petrol, and a motor bicycle does not use much, and I was afraid it was good for a lot more miles. And so it was. It was late now, and we passed no more cars on the road for a long time. I saw moths dance in the light of our lamp and float out again, and sometimes a rabbit frightened by the light and the noise. We seemed all alone in the night with things that could not help me. And then I saw the lights of a car coming towards us, and I called out for help as it passed us. But it was no use. I saw the driver look at me. But he saw that I was alone, or thought that I was alone. How could he have known the awful company that I was in, or even guessed it? And he saw that nothing was following me. So he simply went on. He must have thought I was mad. If this thing spreads he will come on something of the sort himself soon, and I wonder what he will think then. He did nothing to help me. He'll want help himself soon, if this goes on. We all shall. What is going to happen, Ablard?"

"Why do you ask me, Alicia?" he said.

"Because you began it, you know, Ablard," said she.

"When did anyone who started a revolution know where it was going?" he asked. "When did any one of them ever know that it was going to be the end of himself?"

"Oh, Ablard," she said. "But that's not going to happen to you."

"It always has, so far," he said. "But then I didn't start it. I told you I didn't. It was James Watt and Stevenson and Marconi and hundreds of others. I am very late in the field. I've done nothing that's really new. But it's awful to think that I've dragged you into it. What happened after you passed the motor?"

"I was all alone with the thing on a lonely road," said Alicia. "And it was still doing fifty. All I had to do was to prevent it wrecking itself, which I was just able to do. It was quite easy really, because we met nothing for miles. And then I saw lights ahead, those queer lights eyes make in the dark, and I saw that it was a herd of cattle being moved by night. Then I thought this wild rush must end one way or another. I thought the cattle must stop it. You can't go full speed through a herd of cattle with a motor bicycle, or with anything. But the cattle sprang out of the way. I had never seen cattle do that before. They usually get in the way of anything coming towards them. But they seemed to know at once, what I had only gradually felt in my fingers, that this was some new horror; and they were out of its way immediately. It was curious, because they must have seen hundreds of machines, but machines under control of men, and the wild machine on its own they seemed to fear as they never feared us or the things under our control. Their fear of it was so unmistakable that it added to my own terror. It was as though they knew that something would come to the world that was more deadly than Man, and that now it had come."

"Perhaps it was only the noise in the still night that had startled them," I suggested, because she seemed so frightened by some thought that had come to her on that ride through the night.

"No," she said, "they just looked at it and seemed to know, and sprang away at once. It was as though they knew more than I. They showed they knew something was wrong, and the sight of their terror gave reality to my own. I think I could just have steered into one of them, and it would have been softer to hit than the road. But I felt that I couldn't kill a thing that had warned me, for I certainly learned from those cattle that all I had feared was true. Curious their fearing the machine more than us, though we eat them. It was that that made me frightened, Ablard. And I still am. If you've let loose something, Ablard, that cattle dread more than the people who eat them, God help us all."

"It isn't as bad as that, Alicia. We are not beaten yet," said Ablard Pender.

"But what can we do?" said Alicia. "Those cattle were terrified, and so am I."

And he could do no more than repeat: "We are not beaten yet."

"And it wasn't only the cattle," she said.

"What else did you see?" said Pender.

"I won't say anything about moths," said Alicia, "because you would say it was my imagination."

"But why should I?" said Pender.

"About them knowing that something was wrong, I mean," she said. "But it's no use talking about moths, in any case. We know nothing about them. We know that they can communicate over great distances. But I don't know how. So it's no use my trying to say what they knew. But I saw a fox. And it looked at us. We were going along by a hazel wood, and it stood at the edge of it and looked at us, and it showed no fear at all. It had reason enough to fear us: we can't deny that. And when it showed no fear at all, I thought that it must have known that this thing that was rushing past it was not controlled by any of us. Hatred for the machine it shared. I saw its white teeth glaring with it. But it had no fear whatever. It never moved as we passed. Do you think it knew that machines were turning against Man, and that its enemy had a new enemy? It looked like it."

"I don't think it could have known yet, Alicia," said Pender.

"It looked as if it did," she replied. "It looked as if it had no fear of us any longer, and only had hatred for the machine. I can't quite explain to you how it looked, but we seemed to understand each other out there in the night air. And we passed by a field with sheep in it, quite near to the road. I only saw them by flashes, as our light fell on them one by one. And they all had the same look. I never saw sheep look like that before. They seemed to know that I did not control the machine, but was being carried away by it. It was awful to know that they knew it had come to that. They knew it. I could see that they did. I know how Queen Marie Antoinette must have felt being drawn past the crowd on that cart, on her way to the guillotine. I had never thought of it before, but I knew now. I think they knew what was coming. But, oh, Ablard, don't let it come. I think they knew, and that they did not care."

"It will be all right, Alicia," said Pender. "It will be all right. We'll stop it somehow." And he was going on to give her more consolations, such as probably have often been uttered before by helpless people trying to cheer each other on the eve of calamity. But at that moment Samuel Eerith said: "They are coming again, sir." And we listened, and heard a splashing in the marshes, and very soon there was a scratching of metallic things on the door and the window-sill.

"I wish you had let me bring a revolver," I said.

"I told you," said Pender. "It never could penetrate."

"Then what can we do?" I asked.

"It's all right, sir," said Eerith. "They can't get in. They were at it for most of last night, prowling round and scratching."

"What do they want?" I asked Pender.

He took a quick look at Alicia. And then, either to conceal from her that the monster he made threatened her, or simply asking for information, he said to Eerith. "What do you think they are looking for?"

"Oil," said Eerith, "I used to oil them every evening as you told me; but I gave them none yesterday, after the old one wouldn't obey you, sir."

By 'old one' he meant the one that Pender had made himself, the one that had made all the others.

"Do they run on petrol?" I asked with a moment's hope.

"Oh no," said Pender. "It's only lubricating oil. It doesn't make any real difference. They can go fast enough, I'm afraid, without it."

But we heard them moving round the little house like cows at milking time, as though there were something they wanted.

"Will those shutters hold?" I asked. For I heard some of their hands tapping hard against a window-pane.

"The window is too small for them, sir," said Eerith. "They couldn't get through."

'What about the door?' I thought, but said nothing, as such remarks on such occasions have a defeatist air. And Alicia went on with her story.

"After passing the sheep I came on nothing more for a long time that had anything to do with man. I got the idea that animals knew more about what was happening than men did. That motorist that I passed was merely puzzled. But an owl seemed to know. It floated along beside me like a huge feather in a light breeze, or a ghost being drifted away by an early cockcrow, but it kept pace with us for a while, and we were doing a steady fifty. And it gave one hoot and another took it up, and another away over the hills. They seemed to know. Then I was all alone again in the night air, and still the petrol was holding out. I tried to calculate how much would be left, but though my head was clear enough, and was never so clear, it didn't seem to be able to make calculations of that sort. There seemed nothing mathematical about the night. It seemed more like something that owls would understand. Still we came to no water or to anywhere that I would have had a chance of throwing myself off with any hope of surviving. A very sharp turn would have slowed the thing up, but it was a long straight road. I thought of you wondering why I did not come, and wondered what you would think. I knew you would never guess what had happened, and I wondered what you would guess. Then I came to a heath with no hedges, and some gipsies camping near the road, with their big wagon just clear of it. Some of them were still awake, sitting over a fire, cooking something. They looked up and seemed to understand what was happening. I called out to an old woman among them: 'Give me a spell against it.' I don't know if she could have done so. But spells are older than science and I thought she might have. Don't think me very superstitious, Ablard."

I could see that Ablard did, as any scientist would. But he smiled and said nothing.

"And then I saw a badger," Alicia continued. "A thing you never see by day. And I was absolutely certain it knew. Badgers are not so frightened of human beings as all that, and they know all about traffic on roads. But this one was terrified. It started off at once as hard as it could go, and continued running as long as I could see it. There was a bit of a moon by then. I am absolutely certain that it knew that something horrible had got loose. After all, animals do know some things that we don't; and know them at once. Look at the way a dog will know hydrophobia in another dog long before we should say it had broken out. And I am told they can. We should have to go to a vet, and he would have to make all kinds of tests. But a dog knows at once. And look at the way all dogs will leave a city when there is going to be an earthquake next day. They know something awful is coming, and I am sure that badger knew. What is coming, Ablard? Are we going to lose our place in the world? Are machines going to take it? Have they done so already?"

"No, no, Alicia," he said. And she went on with her string of questions.

"But listen to them crawling round here! It is right that we should look after the world? Isn't it, Ablard? Nothing could do it as well as we. Could it? Or have we not used our power properly? Have we enslaved other creatures? We do kill them for food, don't we? Oh, Ablard, we haven't misused our power, have we? We aren't going to be turned out for that, are we?"

"No, no, no, Alicia," he went on saying, but not very convincingly. And the things with their hundred claws went on prowling around the wall, scratching at the door as they passed, and clattering on the path as they crossed it.

CHAPTER XIII

ALL the breakfast we each had was a cup of tea, and with no plans made for escape, or even yet thought of, our minds turned to provisions, and while Alicia continued her story, Samuel Eerith boiled four eggs in a saucepan over his fire.

"I don't know what that badger knew," Alicia went on. "I am afraid it knew that something dreadful was coming. It must have heard thousands of machines going by in the nights, but as our slaves. And now one of them came as the master, and the badger knew. That must mean that it feared the machine more than us. I'm afraid it can't like us, but it must mean that it hates the machine more. When the badger had gone I was all alone with that machine for miles, except for moths and then again an owl. The night air was a help to me: it was like a wonderful drink poured out from a great

fountain. I don't think I could have done it without that
night air. I should have fallen off on to my head, or dropped
dead where I sat.

"Still it went roaring on and still had plenty of petrol. It
was a longer ride than I had ever had. The road was awfully
lonely. Except for the moths. Do you know, I felt that even
they were company of a sort. Anything was company that
was natural. Oh, Ablard, machines are not going to rule the
world, are they?"

"It isn't I that began it, you know, Alicia," he said again.
"I don't know what's going to happen. Nobody ever did,
of all the people that invented machines. They never knew.
But we'll beat them. We'll beat them somehow."

"But how, Ablard?" she said. "How can we do it? They
had such a long start."

"We'll do it, Alicia," he said. "Our enemies always get
a long start, but we'll do it in the end."

But then Samuel Eerith joined in. In times like these
phrases of empty consolation are irritating to some people,
as a paste sandwich would be to a hungry man. He wanted
to hear sense talked; he wanted to hear a plan; he wanted
to know what was to be done. "How are we going to do that,
sir?" he said.

"Well, look how we beat Hitler," said Pender. "We didn't
know how we could do it, but we knew we would. And we did."

"It's worse than Hitler, sir," said Eerith. "He was
human, to some extent."

"We'll do it, Eerith," said Pender.

And there was silence in the room for a while, a silence
that was rather oppressive; and Alicia was looking at Pender
and he had nothing to say. Still we heard those things
splashing and chattering and scratching all round the house.
And to end the awkward silence he said to Alicia: "And then,
Alicia? What happened then?"

"We went on down that road," said Alicia, "and the
main glow of London on our left was now a little behind us,
and we were all alone with the moths. And all of a sudden,

to my intense relief, I saw cats'-eyes. I don't mean real cats' eyes but those glowing things that they put in little pairs all down the middle of a road to tell motors to keep to their left. You have no idea what a relief it was. Because it meant that I was no longer out with this awful thing in absolute loneliness. It meant that we were getting near human beings again, though I didn't know how they could help me. I could never describe to you the terror I felt at being in the power of iron. I would sooner have been the prey of anything that has flesh and blood, even a tiger. I cannot tell you the terror of it. I would rather have been seized by a spectre, or any ghostly thing of the night. Oh, Ablard, even a fiend."

Her young man tried to comfort her. But Alicia went on with her story. "The cats'-eyes were marking out a curve to the left, and we went round the curve, not slow enough to throw myself off. And soon, as far as I could make out, we were heading north instead of east. But the cat's-eyes seemed to indicate a suburb lying ahead. And sure enough we came out of the night lying over miles of countryside into the light of a street, a small street and it was not very light and we were soon through it. Then open spaces again, not quite country and yet not town; places where you would expect to see withered grass by day, and tin cans and old bits of iron and bricks lying about; and after a while a street again, but no traffic to stop us or help me; and I was still in the power of this dreadful thing. There was not a window lit. It was very late now, and everyone but us was asleep. And then one window glowed at the top of a house. It was a wonderful thing to see. It was somebody's home. There were people there. I have always liked to see a window like that in the night; at any time. You may imagine how I yearned towards it now. If I could only have stopped and run into that house, they would have given me help and sympathy. But we rushed on, and we were only a noisy roar in the night to them. And still that petrol held out. Open spaces again, and a gasworks, and more open spaces. And then I came to that street just over there; and it gave a right-angled turn and I saw my chance. And, as the curve slowed it down and forced it close to the kerb, I exerted that slight extra pressure on the steering that I was just able to exert and threw it a couple of inches out of its course and just got it on to the pavement, and there it must have upset. I put out my arms and dived over the handlebars, and I thought I had broken one arm, but I think it's all right, and I saw the thing lying there with its wheels spinning round. And then I ran away from it as hard as I could. But I don't think I need have run, for the horrible thing was like a sheep on its back, and it couldn't get up. And I ran here and hammered at the door, and he very kindly let me in. There was one of those things about, and it moved its head towards me and seemed as if it was listening. But I got in in time. So here we all are. And what do we do now?"

"Now?" said Pender, helpless as those so often are in the presence of revolutions that they have started, either intentionally or merely to exercise an argumentative mind. "Well, all that matters is that you are safe, Alicia."

"But am I?" she said.

"They can't get in here," he answered, and glanced, as he spoke, at the door, at which one of them was at that moment scratching with many of its clawed hands.

"If that horrible one that I made had got you," he went on, seeming to draw some comfort from some disaster not having occurred in the past, instead of trying to conquer whatever threatened the future. But he said no more about that, till Alicia said: "Do you think it was after me."

"I think," said Pender, "that that accursed motor bicycle was bringing you straight to it. I think it was waiting for you at the end of the track." Again he dropped that subject.

"I wish we had a telephone here," said Alicia.

"It would never work if we had," said Pender, "as things are now."

And Pender knew what he was talking about. Many of my readers may or may not remember getting wrong numbers about that time, and hearing humming and other

odd noises, and voices of people to whom they did not wish
to talk. A few of them may have complained, but most,
I expect, were patient. Those that did complain may
remember the cause of it, as it was explained to them in
answer to all complaints. The cause was a technical hitch.
And yet there was something more in it than that, as I think
my story will show. And now Eerith brought us the four
boiled eggs and a loaf of bread and some butter. These
things were very welcome and we all sat down at his long
oak table and had a meal. We of the great race of *homo
sapiens* govern the world by reason, the only creatures
possessed of reason, I have heard, that there are. And yet
how easily are our great plans diverted this way and that by
such things as breakfast. We were all more hopeful now, and
began to plan. First of all there was defence, and what to
do if the worst came to the worst. About this we decided
that if they did break in by the door, we would all get out
by the backdoor, a little door that I had not yet noticed,
expecting that if they did break down the front door they
would all collect there and come pouring in that way,
especially as, according to Pender all except the one he had
made would be deficient in sight, unless they were close to it.
We had two plans then, to be used according to opportunity:
one was to make for the houses, and the other for the Thames,
because these things could not swim and all of us could,
though Alicia was not very good at it, but we were going to
help her. So much for our plans, if the worst came to the
worst. Otherwise we decided to wait for the police, who had
already been told by Pender that something was wrong,
although anything like the full horror of it he had been
unable to tell them so that they understood. And no wonder.
With all the details at my disposal told me by all who wit-
nessed these strange events, and my own personal memories
of what went on in those marshes, it may be found that,
even with all this material, I may have been unable to convince some of my readers that this dreadful revolution against
the authority of mankind ever broke out.

CHAPTER XIV

IN writing this story I need hardly say that I have carefully consulted all who were in close touch with the events concerned in it, or at any rate all of them whom I knew. As the day wore on at Sandyheath and there was still no news of Alicia, and Ablard Pender and I did not return, Mrs. Ingle began to do what most people usually do on such occasions and imagined many ways in which her nephew and Alicia might have died, until having chosen one of them, she filled in its outlines in her mind more and more clearly, until it became to her a reality. Then rather to have a partner in her trouble than to give her much consolation, she telephoned to Alicia's mother, who came over to Sandyheath in her car without any appreciable difficulty in hearing what Mrs. Ingle said on the telephone, and without her car doing any peculiar thing. Evidently the revolution had not spread as far as Kingston. Mrs. Ingle of course knew nothing about the movement starting among those few grim machines against the supremacy of mankind. All she knew was that Alicia had disappeared, and understood at last that her nephew's machine had some frightful power, to which machines had been moving slowly and might not have attained, but for the genius of her nephew, for another twenty or thirty years. That this machine might have something to do with Alicia's disappearance loomed only too ominously among the fears in her mind, and she knew that Ablard Pender had told the police about Alicia. Having no one to talk to about it was driving her to distraction. For it had not occurred to her to talk it all over with Eliza, a leveller head than her own. So that it was a great relief to her when Mrs. Maidston arrived. To Mrs. Maidston's questions about Alicia, Mrs. Ingle could give no answers. She told her that her nephew had gone with me to the marshes and that we had not returned.

G

About this they talked for a long time and I do not know all they said. But the possibility that Ablard Pender's dreadful machine had turned against him was very clear to both of them, although neither of them ever let her imagination range so far as to see that the thing was turning against mankind.

"Hadn't we better get the police to help us?" Mrs. Maidston said after a while.

And Mrs. Ingle agreed, and that idea was a great solace to both of them. Mrs. Ingle telephoned to the inspector to whom her nephew had spoken, and he came round to Sandyheath.

"What news?" asked Mrs. Ingle as he came in.

"We have got her motor bicycle," said the inspector.

This did not mean that the police were within half a mile of us. It only meant that one policeman, seeing a motor bicycle on the pavement had reported it to his police-station, so that inquiries being sent out by the police at Kingston were very soon met by information identifying the cycle, though there was still no news of Alicia; nor was this clue followed up for some time, at any rate in the right direction, for the difficulty that Ablard Pender had had in explaining to the police that a live and hostile monster of iron was lurking in those marshes with several others had delayed any search for Alicia in that direction. The theories on which the police were working at first were still too human. If she had wished to escape from her home, it was not to the marshes that she was likely to run. In their experience it was always to something brighter and far more populous that a girl would go. Abduction seemed to them far more probable; but in case of abduction they could not get out of their minds the human element, and they wasted all the morning searching for evidence of some man. And now at Sandyheath the inspector was addressing repeated inquiries to the two women about all the men that Alicia knew, while others of the police force were making inquiries of all lonely men seen the night before on the roads that Alicia had taken. For besides having been identified at two red lights that her rebellious machine had ignored, she had been noticed at one or two other points, though the number of her machine had not been actually noted there. Also the driver of the car to whom she had called for help had reported to the police that a girl had done so.

"May I ask," said the inspector, "if Miss Maidston is related to Mr. Pender in any way?"

"Oh no," said one of the women, Mrs. Maidston I think, "but they are engaged to be married."

"And we have to ask all kinds of questions," said the inspector.

"Of course," said both of them.

"Then may I ask just one question more?" he said.

"Certainly," said Mrs. Maidston.

"But why not?" said Mrs. Ingle.

"Was there ever any mental illness in either of the families?"

"No, nothing of the kind," and "certainly not," came from the two ladies.

"Only a little excitement sometimes," said the inspector.

And this they both denied. But the denial helped to form the inspector's opinion that there was something a little queer in both families. For Mrs. Ingle, who had noticed the inspector's questions drifting away for some while from her own appreciation of the case, whatever that may have been, was certainly considerably excited by the question that indicated that her nephew as well as Alicia, and even herself, were off their heads.

"Those are only questions we have to ask as a matter of form," said the inspector. "It does not mean we have any preconceived opinions. We are not allowed to have any preconceived opinions."

Then Mrs. Ingle and Mrs. Maidston knew that nothing her nephew had said at the police-station or that they had told the inspector had been able to convey any idea of what danger menaced Alicia, or that there was any possibility of any threat to the supremacy of the human race. That such a threat existed Mrs. Ingle knew now, reluctant though she had been for so long to recognize that her dull and studious nephew could have set in motion anything that could affect the destinies of mankind. How much Mrs. Maidston knew I was never told, but there is no doubt that Alicia had passed on to her some intuitive knowledge she had of Pender's power, even before her motor bicycle had shown her such dreadful proof of it. And now, the difficulty with which the two ladies had to struggle was that, to a man who had already some doubt of their sanity, they had to explain that a man whom that doubt also shadowed had made a brain out of metal that was superior to human brains, and every moment they wasted explaining this were moments wasted in the search for Alicia, during which the police would be seeking diligently, but all along the wrong trails. What could they do? Mrs. Maidston began to humour the inspector, but as that could only be done by agreeing with him that Ablard Pender was a little fanciful, and even that Mrs. Ingle had been a trifle excited, it got them no further; this brought them no nearer to making the inspector guess what might have happened, and meanwhile Alicia was lost, and sinking further and further, as both these ladies feared, into the power of the dreadful machines. The rational methods of the police had already produced a good deal, having traced Alicia over much of her terrible journey. But the wild fears of the girl's mother and Mrs. Ingle could only give information that was leading the inspector to consider them mad. And then he asked a few formal questions again, and they were as far as ever from discovering the fate of Alicia, and further still from finding her. It seemed a hopeless impasse, when the inspector, looking for further evidence, inquired who else was in the house, and was told of Eliza. Questioning the housemaid seemed a small task to the inspector; but he asked to see her, and Mrs. Ingle rang the bell in the drawing-room, and Eliza came in. She came in among the fears of the two ladies and the theories of the inspector like a north wind among leaves. To the first question of the inspector about the occupations of Ablard Pender she replied with vigour: "Don't you think that that gentleman doesn't know what he is doing. More than he knows himself perhaps." (Whatever she meant by that.) "He's made a machine that's more like the devil than anything that hasn't horns and a tail. And I'd sooner deal with the devil, if you ask me, than deal with it."

In this rush of words the inspector clutched at his note-book as they say drowning men do at straws, and tried to steady things by asking his formal questions.

"A machine, you say?" he asked.

"Yes," said Eliza. "And cleverer than you, and wickeder than any man."

In all conflicts it is energy that counts, and the inspector who till a few moments ago was dominating the drawing-room by his assurance and his authority, was now clutching his theories that seemed in danger of being swept away by Eliza. Reason said to him the woman is mad like the rest of them. But energy is stronger than reason, and Eliza dominated now where a while ago he had dominated.

"And with things like that about," went on Eliza, "do you wonder we lost Miss Alicia?"

"Perhaps, Eliza," said Mrs. Ingle in the last effort she made on behalf of the inspector. But Eliza swept on. "It's that machine that has done it," she said.

"What machine?" said the inspector.

"The machine Mr. Pender made," went on Eliza.

"A machine?" said the inspector. "What does it do exactly? Does it cut the lawn, or——"

"It can think," said Eliza.

The inspector scratched his head. Then he wrote several lines in his note-book, saying no more. And then he said: "I think that will be all," and walked out of the room and out of the house. But Eliza would not let him rest. She ran after him, and on the gravel outside the door said: "We want to find Miss Alicia."

"Yes, yes," said the inspector. "We are looking for her."

"We want to find her," said Eliza. "And you won't find her if you don't get after that machine which has caused all the trouble. I tell you it's a thing like the devil. And twice as clever."

"Yes, yes," said the inspector and walked quickly away.

"And it's got Miss Alicia," she called after him.

Something in the woman's assurance, something perhaps in the mere tone of her voice, certainly nothing that seemed reasonable in what she said, had caused the inspector to stop and turn round and, still within hearing of Mrs. Ingle, who told me about it when I questioned her later, he asked: "Where is this machine?"

"It's in the marshes along the Thames," she said. "South bank. And a lot more of them. And if you don't get at them you'll never find Miss Alicia."

"Machines?" said the inspector.

"Yes, machines. And able to think," said Eliza.

"Have you seen these machines, as you call them?" he asked.

"Seen one of them," said Eliza. "And I know there's a lot of others."

"How do you know?" asked the inspector.

"How do I know?" said Eliza. "Do you think a housemaid doesn't know what's going on in a house? And I've been here five years. There's things go on here that would puzzle you. But never mind that. You've got to find Miss Alicia."

"And you say she's where the machines are," said the inspector, "along the Thames?"

"Yes, in the marshes," said Eliza. "And you'll have to smash those machines, or you won't get her from them. And Mr. Pender says bullets can't do it. They're too tough."

Before the inspector asked his next question he glanced over his shoulder towards the road; for at any moment a policeman might have been coming for him to give him further information, and he did not wish to be overheard talking with this woman about machines that could think, and that had caught a girl in some marshes. There was nobody there, and he said: "Those machines that are too strong for bullets, and that you say have got Miss Alicia Maidston; how can they be broken up if they are as hard as you say?"

I think that something in the vehemence of Eliza had lured him half-way to believing her; or perhaps only a quarter of the way. But, if he had been overheard, I am certain he would have explained that he was testing the woman's sanity.

"Simple enough," said Eliza. "You must ask the Air Force to help you. Bomber squadron would deal with them all right."

"I don't think," said the inspector, "that the Royal Air Force would take advice from a lady on a matter of that sort."

"Good lord," said Eliza. "Do you think I don't know what thousand-pound bombs are like? I have seen 'em. And they'd do the trick nicely."

"Thousand-pound bombs!" said the inspector and walked away. But at the gate by the little rhododendron, he met the odd man Ewens, who looked after the kitchen-garden. And something that Ewens said to him seemed to have given him some idea that the two educated women were unable to make him see, something, whatever it was, that may have altered the whole course of the line that was taken by the police.

CHAPTER XV

THE day wore on in the little house in the marshes, and very soon we got hungry again. Luckily Samuel Eerith had a good ham, with only about a quarter taken out of it, and this he gave us and some more bread; and, just as he put our four plates on the table, we heard silence fall outside the house and knew the machines had gone. Anything that they did was ominous, as must always be the case with the actions of any enemy that is of superior intellect. One cannot hope that such an enemy has overlooked some simple thing, and can only conclude that, whatever he may be doing, it is something that bodes no good. But whatever their action boded in all withdrawing, some of our watchful attention was a little distracted now by the sight of the ham, and we were given a valuable opportunity also to replenish our store of water; for we did not know how long we might have to stay in the cottage. First of all of course we looked out to see how far they had gone, so as to decide if we could get Alicia to the safety of one of the houses in the street from which she had escaped from her motor bicycle. But there was one of them out there watching between us and the houses; and our other possible route of escape, through the marshes by way of the Thames, seemed altogether inadvisable when we could not see where the rest of them were. Whether the one that was watching was one that the monster had made and therefore, according to Pender, blind, or whether it was his monster itself, we could not see. But, even if it were one of the blind ones, we dared not risk its acute hearing picking up our steps on the path, or splashing through the water beside it; but all of us went to the water-barrel, and gradually rotated it till we got it to the door and with some difficulty up a step and into the house. Still the watcher remained in its place, and the others were out of sight. There was little opportunity for words while we struggled with the barrel, but now that we had got it into the house and locked the door again and were all four of us sitting at the oak table, Alicia asked Ablard Pender: "What do you think they are doing?"

And he had the sense to give no empty reassurance, but admitted he did not know. And we all started guessing, and not one of our guesses came near the simple and horrible truth. And then we gave up guessing and settled down to eat ham, for we were very hungry.

"They can't get in," said Samuel Eerith.

And we glanced at the large amount of ham that was left, and two loaves of bread and three or four pounds of butter on a shelf beside packets of sugar and tea, and we ate our lunch in content, even although we knew that the departure of the monsters was the result of no idle pique, but part of some plan they were working out, and that it boded no good. Still we were glad of it, for beside the respite it gave us, and the opportunity to replenish our drinking water, every hour that passed we hoped would bring rescue closer. In what form it might come we had no idea, nor how things that bullets were unable to penetrate could be even attacked, but we would not give up hope for any inability to see how help could come. Later on we looked out once again towards the edge of the town, but the solitary monster was still between us and it, and somewhere in the marshes between us and the Thames all the others were hidden.

"Can't we get away?" asked Alicia.

But Pender said: "No, we can't risk it. Help is bound to arrive."

But there was no sign of help coming. Pender was right; but Alicia's terrible experience, that, so far as I know, nobody had ever quite had before, had made her over-anxious, and impatient of the presence of these monsters, wherever they were.

"Help will come," said Pender. "I have told the police. And the presence of your motor bicycle on the pavement alone would set them looking for something."

But help did not come. That long summer day wore on, and the evening cries of birds began to wail over the marshes. And, melancholy though those cries may be, they cheered us as we sat drinking tea in the slowly darkening room, for they were the sounds of natural things, sounds of the ancient regime that still existed in spite of the revolution that now seemed to have come to a head, which threatened to free the world from the rule of Man, to hand it over to the power of a tyranny so much worse. Still the monsters came no nearer.

Still between us and the houses, whenever we peeped, the lonely monster was watching. We began to guess once more over the tea-cups what the other monsters were doing. But after several guesses we turned to Pender and asked him what he thought, and he said: "They are cleverer than I. I do not know." And that rather ended our guessing.

It was silent in the cottage after that, and rather chilly, though it was in the month of June, and we all sat round the fire at which Eerith had boiled the eggs, and the room grew dimmer and dimmer. And just as darkness descended over the marshes and the black shapes of the plover went wailing across the sky, just visible against streaks that were left by day, we saw a light in the loneliness and the darkness, and it was moving towards us.

"Help at last," said Alicia. "But why is it coming from there?"

We still kept the door locked, but we had opened the shutters, and now we all went to the window from which Alicia was watching.

"It must be a lantern," said Alicia. "And somebody is coming to help us."

"I don't like it coming that way," said Pender. "Those things have turned against us. I think we ought to warn whomever it is. He is too near them." And he went to the door.

"Wait a minute," I said. "Supposing it isn't a man."

"Supposing what?" said Pender.

"Supposing it isn't a man," I said again. "It's keeping rather level, you know. It's not bobbing up and down like a man walking. And it's coming rather fast."

"It is," said Pender. "And there's two more of them. Three more I see now. And they are certainly level and fast. It must be machines of some sort. Or some of them."

"It's them right enough," said Eerith.

"Then they can make fire," I said.

"Seems so," said Eerith.

"Yes, that's it," said Pender.

"I'm not going to let them burn down my cottage," said Eerith, "if that's what they want to do."

"How can we stop them?" asked Pender.

"Easy enough," Eerith answered, as he ran to the door. "I'm going to get all the moss and wet things that I can before they come, and slam 'em against my door. Hand me that basin, sir, if you will, while I unlock it."

And Pender brought him a basin that there was on a dresser, and Eerith took it and went out, and the rest of us ran out with him, and the lights were still some way off over the marshes, but coming nearer, and I noticed three more of them. The water came very close to Samuel Eerith's doorstep, and he easily filled his basin and threw water over the door, while we gathered handfuls of wet moss from the marshes all round. What particularly helped was a hammer and nails which Eerith got from indoors and gave to Alicia, and she nailed the bits of wet moss to the door, while Eerith threw several more basins of water over it. But the lights were getting too near for us to do any more work outside, and we ran in and locked the door, and Eerith began boring holes through it with a gimlet. He had one of those things that squirt out a stream of chemicals in order to put out fire. Many houses have them, and they are good things to have. It stood on a bracket that was clamped to the wall near his fireplace.

"While I can get the nozzle of this through one of them holes," he said, "they'll not burn my door."

Then he ran out of his backdoor and threw water over that too, as there were no lights to be seen on that side. But we called to him to come back, as the things were getting close now, and we could hear them closing in on the front door, all of them carrying burning pieces of wood, as we could see from the window where we took a last look before closing the shutters, and I counted a dozen by then. There was no other wood they could get at except the window-sill. Then they came squelching right up to the door out of the marshes on to the bit of dry land by the doorstep. The marshes were no deeper than a few inches, and they kept their bodies well out of the water by walking with their legs or arms or whatever you call them, stretched at full length, as we saw by the light of the pieces of burning wood. But, peeping through one of the holes that Eerith had bored in the door, I saw that their bodies were quite close to the ground, like what they always seemed to me, huge beetles.

"They're up to the door," I shouted to Eerith.

"They won't burn my door now," he said.

"But the thatch," I called out. For we had not thought of that. It may seem an odd oversight, but we'd plenty to think of, and odder things than come most people's way in a lifetime.

"They can't reach it," said Pender.

"Can they throw?" I asked.

"No," he said.

"But the sparks from the fire," said Alicia.

And they were heaping up their burning faggots against the door as she spoke.

"I've house-leeks on my roof," said Eerith.

"House-leeks?" she said.

"Yes, miss," he answered. "Haven't you ever heard that a house that has house-leeks never burns?"

"No," said Alicia.

"It's an old saying," he said, "miss. And them old sayings has had time to be proved wrong. But they never have been. I trust them. I wouldn't have had any fire-extinguishers here. I'd trust house-leeks. But Mr. Pender put one in, and we can use it to stop them doing any harm to the door. I threw a basin of water on to the edge of the thatch just over the door to moisten the moss, but it was moist enough already. It's half of it moss."

"Yes," I said. "I noticed your thatch looked very black."

"It's the moss," he said. "That will never burn. But it's the old saying I trust. I trust all of them. They've come down a long way."

"Your house must be very damp," said Alicia.

"Damp?" said Eerith. "Not a bit of it, miss. It only keeps it warm. Warm in winter and cool in summer."

Alicia glanced at the dark stains of damp that had crept down the wall of the room, wide at the top near the thatch and narrowing as they went downwards, and would have said something more to Eerith. But now the crackle of burning faggots was heard against the door, above the sound of the scratching of metallic claws upon it, and it was time to turn to the door. Eerith filled his basin from the water-butt and threw the water under the door, and we heard the hiss as it went right into the fire, and then he threw out another. Meanwhile Pender put the nozzle of the fire-extinguisher through one of the holes that Eerith had drilled, and let some of it trickle down the outside of the door and on to the fire. It prevented the fire from getting a good start, and it had not yet got hold of the door, but it was still alight, and right against the house, and Eerith looked a little uneasy. I picked up a poker: it seemed the only weapon we had. But Eerith said to Pender then: "I never did any poaching in the marshes, sir; shooting ducks and that kind of thing, as some people do who have no right to."

"No, I'm sure you didn't," said Pender.

"I never did, sir," he said. "But at one time I was much troubled by rats, and I had the offer of a gun cheap, from a man who had given up shooting, and I got it for them. I knew you wouldn't mind me shooting a rat now and then, sir."

"No, of course not," said Pender.

And Eerith brought a twelve-bore out of a cupboard and a bagful of cartridges. "I only had it for rats, sir," he repeated.

"It can't penetrate steel," Pender told him.

"No, sir," said Eerith, "but it can smash those fingers of theirs."

"Yes, it could do that," said Pender.

Then he went to the door and used some more of the fire-extinguisher.

"Their fire's not doing well," he said, and he put his hand flat on the door. "There is no heat here. Better go to the backdoor and listen. They might try there."

I went, and all was quiet at the backdoor.

But it was to the window they went, when they found that the front door would not catch fire; and we heard them lifting up faggots against the frame. Then Eerith opened the shutters and the window as well, and fired at an iron hand that was reaching up with a faggot. The thing dropped the faggot, and the sight cheered Alicia. I saw it fall right past the window. But Pender said to Eerith: "How many cartridges have you?"

"Fifty more, sir," said Eerith.

"They have each of them got about a hundred hands," said Pender.

And on top of this depressing remark one of the iron pairs of claws clutched Eerith's gun as he was aiming out of the window, and pulled it out of his hands. He fired both barrels, before the thing got it; but he hit nothing.

"Now what can we do?" asked Alicia.

"It doesn't matter," said Pender. "The thing was no use against them. They still can't get in." And he went up with the fire-extinguisher to the open window.

"Many's the time I've stood at the window at night," said Eerith, "to throw a basin of water over tom cats that came after my puss yowling. And a horrid noise they made. I never thought I should have these things trying to get in."

"Why! It's the very thing!" shouted Pender.

"What is?" asked Alicia.

"Guns are no good," said Pender. "But throw water over them. Aim at that kind of a neck that I gave them. Throw it as you did over the cats. It can get in from the top, and it will rust those wires."

"What wires?" said Alicia.

"All those fine wires that make their brains," said Pender. "Wires along which all their impulses run. Like thoughts in our brains. It will rust them."

Hand after hand was reaching up flaming sticks to the window-sill, which was beginning to catch alight. There was not room for them to get through the window; but if the frame burned away there might be. And then Eerith began throwing basins of water over their backs, running to his barrel and refilling the basin from it. One could see that they did not like the water. But it had no effect on them. It had an effect on the window-sill, however. For Eerith had dodged back into the room to avoid the steel claws, and some of the water fell on the burning window-sill. There must have been a dozen of them there, but each of them moved away as it got the water over its back, and soon they were all out of range of water from Eerith's basin. Then Pender used some more of the fire-extinguisher, and got the sill well saturated and put the fire out, and still had some of the chemical left. The flames from the faggots that the monsters were carrying began to die down, so that we could not begin to see where they were. But we knew well enough that they were crouching quite close to the house, and watching us.

"Cut open those cartridges," said Pender to Eerith, "and put them in water. They've got the gun and, if they ever forced a way in, they would shoot us before we could get away, if they found those cartridges."

"But they couldn't do that," I said.

"I tell you," said Pender, "they are more intelligent than I. And don't you remember what happened to you when you played chess against that thing? They've seen the gun fired and they've got two empty cartridges in it. It won't take a quick intelligence long to see how to load it. Get into your head that they can out-think all of us. We are lost if we don't realize that."

"What will they do now?" I asked.

And Alicia looked at Pender, waiting for his answer.

"They might easily try to starve us out," he said. "But they'd have to wait a long time for their oil if they did that, and I hope the police will come some time. I think it would suit them better to go back and get a lot more wood, wherever they get it from, and pile it up against both doors and the window, and. . . ."

But he looked at Alicia and said no more, evidently not wishing to alarm her, and I don't know what else he thought the monsters might do. And it seemed to be as Pender had said, for we heard no sound of the monsters all that night, and nothing disturbed the silence of the marshes any more, except the hoots of one owl that sailed over them hunting, and hunted away out of hearing. None of us slept that night.

CHAPTER XVI

ALL that night the iron monsters must have been collecting logs from some distance away. For we heard no more of them that night. But when the birds began to awake and to wail over the marshes, Eerith saw from the window a movement among the rushes, and called our attention, and Pender and I saw a long line of bundles of wood crawling towards us. It was the monsters with all the logs they could carry on their backs, held there by their clusters of hands, and not alight. It was clear that they were going to pile them against the house, and obvious that when the whole heap was alight the place would be uninhabitable: doors and windows would go, and even the wet thatch. Pender and Eerith and I said nothing, not wishing to alarm Alicia. Though what good that was I could not think, considering how soon the thing that we feared seemed likely enough to come down on us. They came on closer with their great bundles of wood, with their legs straight and stiff to keep them out of the water. And as soon as they came to the dry land beside the house they divided into three groups, and one lot ran up to the front door and threw down their logs against it, and another group ran round to the backdoor, and we heard the logs they threw down thumping against that, while another lot piled their logs up under the window. I looked at Pender, to see what he thought of doing; but his expression was blank and I turned to Eerith. Eerith went and filled his basin without a word and came back to the window and opened it, having put his basin down. Then he lifted the basin and threw the contents of it over the back of one of the monsters, and it scuttled at once out of range. Clawed hands came through the window, trying to catch him; but he soused two more of them in spite of that, and each of them slithered away.

"They don't like it no more than them tom cats did," he said.

But they managed to pile the logs up under the window and, what was worse, they had brought a bundle of straw. And then we saw a puff of smoke in the distance, and knew that another was coming along with fire.

"We might have to run for it," I said in a low voice to Pender.

"She would be torn to pieces," he answered.

And I saw that that would be bound to happen, because they were faster than any of us, and Alicia would be the slowest. There would be no chance of her reaching the houses. I saw that Pender was right.

"We will have to stay," I said.

"Yes," he answered. "Though that seems no better."

It was one of those black moments in life when there seems no way out.

"Look," said Eerith.

He was looking away from the monsters towards the town. And we looked and saw three cars, full of men, coming along the pathway that led from the town.

"It's the police," I said.

"At last," said Pender.

But at that moment the front car started skidding from side to side, in a way I had never quite seen a car skid before. And then the two behind it behaved as oddly. And then they all stopped dead.

H

"They've stopped," said Pender.

"Never mind, sir," said Eerith. "The policemen are getting out."

And so they were. And they were all coming towards us. And soon I saw to my surprise that they had what the police so rarely have in England, for they all carried revolvers. I was all the more astonished by this because I had gathered clearly from Pender that he had quite failed to explain to the inspector at Kingston that these dreadful machines were threatening mankind, or even that there were such machines, or that machinery, however long it maintains the frightful rate of its recent progress, would ever be able to do so. As much as the inspector believed that the law was superior to burglary, so he believed that the human race was superior to anything else that there is, or anything else that could be. He had never noticed the increasing power of machinery; and, if he had, he would not have considered that it could ever threaten mankind. He no more thought of the possibility of the revolution now under way in those marshes, than emperors long overthrown had thought of it when they gave rights to favoured subjects and their heirs after them for ever. I did not know, and do not know now, what Ewens had said to the inspector in the gateway of Sandyheath by the little rhododendron as he walked away. Whatever it was, it must have altered the inspector's whole point of view, as a simple sentence sometimes may, where whole arguments fail, and he had set in motion the most extreme steps the police ever take and had gone to the length of arming a dozen men. Of the full menace that Pender had rashly let loose on the world he could not know anything; that would have been too much for any man's imagination to grasp after a single talk with a scientist, whose whole language was strange to him. But he took the amplest measures he could, not dreaming that revolvers, which were supplied with some reluctance, would be utterly futile against this rebellion of iron.

We saw the policeman coming along the path towards

us, all with their revolvers in their hands, evidently well prepared, black heavy revolvers that looked like ·450s, which they turned out to be. Then we saw several of the monsters turning their heads towards them all at the same moment, as though obeying one impulse. And then we saw one of them leave the rest and rush at the police. It went over the marshes faster than a man running. All the rest stayed near their logs by our two doors, and round the one window just out of range of the water from Eerith's basin, which they disliked as much as the tom cats had done. We wondered why more of them did not attack the police, but decided that they were so eager for oil that they would not leave the cottage, in which they knew that Eerith had two or three drums of it. As the horrible machine went for the police they spread out quickly and opened fire at once, and we heard the ricochets scream through the air off the iron back of the monster. But the bullets had no effect upon it whatever, and it came up with the police as quick as a fox upon chickens, and seized one of them with its claws. If a dozen of them had attacked, they could have killed every policeman. As it was, all the rest of them rushed at the thing and, when they saw that firing had no effect, they beat its arms with truncheons and, when the truncheons broke, they hammered it with their revolvers and beat off some of its claws and threw some of its joints out of gear, and just managed to save the man upon whom it had sprung. Then they came on towards us, and the thing that had attacked them stood glowering at them for a while, till it was recalled to the rest by the queer termite-like influence of the monster that Pender had made. There was a tremendous clamour and scrimmage at the front door. The batons of the police were all broken already, and even their revolvers used as bludgeons would never have got them through; but they picked up some of the logs that the monsters had brought and used them against those clutching arms. And, as all machinery, however strong, is delicate, they smashed a great many of the arms and the claws; and, as Eerith opened the door at

the right moment, they were all able to rush in before the
monsters got any of them. I was afraid that an experience so
horrible and so new must have very greatly upset them; and
Pender said as much, being even more conscious about them
than I, as he knew that he was responsible for the whole of
this dreadful uprising of metal against mankind. But one of
them said to him: "Oh, we don't mind it for being new, sir.
Poor old Goering used to play some nasty new tricks on us.
But we soon got used to them."

Eerith shut the door as soon as the last man got in,
slamming it against the nose of one of the monsters, and
locked it. And Alicia bandaged the man who had been
caught by those iron claws, which had left deep rips down
his shoulder-blades when he so nearly shared the fate of the
dog that Pender's monster had caught. They did not unduly
mind the attack because it was new, but they were certainly
puzzled by it, and we now had the job of explaining the
situation to them, which of course it had been impossible for
anybody to do when none of them had seen these horrible
things at work, or known that such work or such things
were possible. When Alicia had bandaged the injured man,
the next thing that she did, with Eerith's help, was to make
tea for all of us. Obviously provisions could not long hold
out now, but we had enough tea for a dozen more men, and
some left over.

We could hear the monsters piling back the logs against
the front door; and, looking out of the window, we saw that
smoke from the burning log was still some distance away,
and the monster that carried it seemed to be coming slower
than the speed at which these things were accustomed to
travel. So before we made any more plans Pender very
rightly began to explain to the police over our cups of tea
what it was we should have to make plans about. With the
support of all of us acquiescing in all he said, and speaking
to men who had seen what they just had seen, the explanation was very much more easily made than when in a police-
station in a suburban street, unaffected by any disturbance,

he was trying to explain that something menaced humanity,
which, though it had gradually been coming upon us for
years, no one had ever yet noticed. We brought up an old
arm-chair to the table for the wounded man, and Eerith
got two of them to drag in his bed from his small bedroom
that opened out of the end of the room, and which was the
only other room in the house, besides a small pantry. The
bed was put along one side of the table, and four of them sat
on that, and there were wooden chairs for five or six more,
and some sat on a bolster and pillows on the floor, and one
sat on a box. And Eerith found cups or drinking vessels of
some sort for all of us.

"It's like this," said Pender. "Machines have been getting
cleverer for many years."

"Cleverer?" repeated the inspector in charge.

"Well, whatever you like to call it," said Pender. "They
can calculate, they can hand you your change, they can make
most of the things that we use, they can do the most astonishing things. Take a torpedo alone: it drops into the sea, it
rights itself, it swims along a few feet under the surface,
keeping exactly the right level; if it missed, as it used sometimes to do in the old days, it dived to the bottom of the sea
so as to be out of harm's way: now it doesn't even miss, it
turns towards the ship on its own. And look at the anti-
aircraft shells that explode when they get near the aeroplane
that they are after, that explode exactly at the right distance
from it. Look at the watches that chime the time for you, as
well as show the time with their hands. Well, I won't go on;
you have only to observe. Machines have been doing the
most wonderful things, and every year more and more
wonderful. They were gradually catching us up, doing everything we were able to do. Now they have got past us. You
saw what those machines were able to do."

"I understand you made them, sir," said the inspector.

"I made one of them, certainly," said Pender. "It made
the rest. But you mustn't think I started all this. I only
gave a helping hand, as a lot of other people were doing.

We never meant to start a revolution. We never knew it would come. We didn't even know that it could come. I am as much surprised by it as any of you. I didn't know how devilish machines could be when they had the power. We might have seen it by looking at the soulless things that they made. There were people sitting on iron bars in their houses instead of the graceful chairs that used to be carved from mahogany. Houses were being made like large black packing-cases, without ornament, without decoration, without any human fancy blossoming on them in wreaths or wings or leaves, because the machine has no such fancies and it was elbowing the spirit of Man out of the way.

"This is the last revolution. If you can't stamp it out now, there'll be no other chance for mankind. You must get that into your head. The last revolution. You must understand that, if we lose our place, we can never get back."

"Look out, sir," said Eerith. "That thing's coming with the burning wood."

And the inspector and I looked out of the window, and sure enough the thing that carried the lighted log was getting near. But it was coming very slowly. I glanced at Eerith and saw what I had noticed before, that he had moved rather stiffly as he went to the window. Indeed, all his movements were a little stiff, as one often sees with any man who has lived all his life beside marshes. And suddenly the idea came to me from seeing Eerith, that this monster also was getting stiff and slow. It also had been splashing about in the marshes; and it wanted oil and could not get it. But, however slow it came, it was getting near now, and there was the bundle of straw under the faggots waiting for it by the front door. The inspector told Eerith to bore some much larger holes in both doors, and this he did, beginning with the front door, because that was the one towards which the monster was coming.

Luckily they were all at the front door, and, thanks to the slowness of the one that was bringing the fire, Eerith had time to bore three loop-holes; and the inspector and two of

his men went to them just as the thing came out of the water
and waddled towards the door. The sights of several of the
revolvers had been knocked all askew in the fight with the
monster that had seized the man, but the ones that they took
to the loop-holes were still in good condition and rapid
firing broke out, very noisy in a small room. I wondered
what they were doing, knowing that bullets were of no use
against these monsters. And then one of the men shouted
"got it!" And it turned out that they had been shooting at
the piece of burning timber with which the monster had
been going to set light to the straw, and had knocked it out
of its hand.

It ran at once to where the stick was burning, but the
police had been able to get a good aim at it as it lay on the
ground and, as soon as the thing picked it up, they knocked
it out of its hands again. This went on for some while, and
the stick was only smouldering by the time that the monster
got it up to the straw, and then another one of the police
hit it with a stream from the fire-extinguisher, which also
went over the straw. And then one of those long thin arms
came through the largest hole in the door, right at a policeman's face; but he stepped back in time and hit at it with a
log that they had brought into the house. Another arm,
whether of the same monster or one of the others, slipped
through another hole, swinging and groping about, and
fared no better. Eerith meanwhile was boring holes in the
backdoor. The monster that had tried to set fire to the straw
then turned round and went back over the marshes, and two
or three others went with it.

"Going for more fire," said the inspector.

"Yes, that must be it," said Pender.

"Where do they get it?" the inspector asked.

"I don't know," said Pender. "Somewhere beyond the
marshes."

"Haven't they matches?"

"Evidently not," said Pender. "And they have not got
the sulphur to make them with. Either they must have raided

a house and got the fire from there, or they get it by chipping flints, which they won't find just round here, but there are plenty of them in the gravel nearer the Thames."

"Fire seems their difficulty," the inspector said.

"Well, you see, sir," said Eerith, looking round from the backdoor, "I always used to light their furnaces, and they got accustomed to me doing it for them. They never had to bother about making fire. They're clever enough, them things, and could make matches easier than you or me. But Mr. Pender says they don't have no sulphur."

"No," said Pender, "they can't get that. They must be going to get more lighted sticks now from over there."

And we noticed that all three of them were going a bit slow.

"Is there any chance of reinforcements coming?" asked Pender.

"We can call them up," said the inspector. "We have one of those walkie-talkies with us."

And he spoke to one of his men, who was carrying the wireless instrument, and gave him a message which he repeated into it.

"I don't think it will work," said Pender, "here."

"Why not?" said the inspector.

And then the man with the instrument said: "I don't seem to be getting through, sir."

"No," said Pender. "You wouldn't."

"What is it?" asked the inspector.

"It's only that they are as clever as Marconi," said Pender. "Or as any man. What we can do, they can do."

"But I can hardly believe it," the inspector said.

"We mustn't be too surprised," Pender replied. "We weren't much surprised by our own wonders, when wireless came and all that. Only we got the idea that there was nothing cleverer than ourselves. And all the while there was the queen termite-ant, which could do all that Marconi could. I am not sure that we were the cleverest things in the world even then. And we are certainly not now."

"Can you get it to work?" the inspector asked the man with the walkie-talkie.

"No, sir," said the policeman.

"Then I suppose they can do it," said the inspector to Pender. "But more of our men will come up just the same. They know we're here, and the firing must have been heard."

"Then you must signal to them to keep away, as soon as they come in sight, and tell them to get artillery."

"Artillery?" said the inspector.

"Yes," replied Pender. "Bullets can't stop them. You've seen that."

"But we can't ask the War office to send us artillery," the inspector said.

"You must get it," Pender told him, "and stop this revolution. These things have got out of hand. I could control them once, and I can't any longer. I was only doing what everyone else was doing, helping machines to grow stronger and stronger, and thinking I was doing good to mankind. I have made my mistake. But I see it now, and I want you to see it. I am just like a slave-owner of old days who has imported slaves for years; and one day they turn against him. Such a man would ask for help. But I am asking for help for the human race."

"The human race?" said the inspector.

"Yes," said Pender. "I tell you it's the last revolution."

We were all back at the little table now, except one of them who was watching at the window, and one at the front door, looking through the holes that Eerith had bored at the monsters that were all squatting there in a semicircle, evidently waiting for the others to come back with more fire. We were seated again and all listening to Pender.

"It is the last revolution," he repeated. "I am a scientist and I have studied geology, as well as this business that I wish I had never put my hand to, and you must take my word for it: no race in the long story of Earth that was ever superseded ever got back. We are not the first strong race that the earth has known. If we go under now, we shall go the way of the mammoth and the great lizards, and machines will dominate everything."

"If we go under now?" said the inspector. "It doesn't look as if they could do that."

"No revolution," said Pender, "looked like doing it at the start. All of them might have been stopped, if taken in time. We must stop this one."

While Pender was speaking I noticed that the wounded man in the arm-chair was staring at me with that intensity of gaze that denotes a high temperature, and I called Alicia's attention to him, and we took him away to the bedroom, and brought the mattress and blankets and sheets and pillows back to it, and laid him on them and undressed him and looked at the long gashes again which the monster had ripped in his back, and found them inflamed; and Alicia renewed the dressings, which she had made out of all our handkerchiefs, and made the wounded man as comfortable as she could in the bed. There was only a skylight, cut in the thatch, to light the bedroom; and, as Pender assured us that the things could not climb, this did not have to be guarded. Several of us looked out of the window from time to time, as well as the man on watch there, but we saw no sign of the three returning with fire. Still the others watched by the front door.

"What do they want to get in here for so much?" asked the inspector.

"Two reasons," said Pender. "Jealousy and oil."

"Jealousy?" the inspector repeated.

"Yes," Pender answered. "I made the things as perfect as I could. And they are perfect mechanically. But I could not avoid frailties. And there's nothing like any human spirit in them to control the frailties they have. I suppose the one that I made is nearest to being human, though it's a long long way from it, and the others are further still. It's jealous, you see, of Miss Maidston, and it's brought all the rest to help kill her. That's one thing they want to do."

"The War Office might possibly help us if it was to save life," said the inspector.

"It isn't to save one or two lives," said Pender. "It's to stop the revolution that will make slaves of mankind. I tell you, if they win we will never get back. It is the last revolution."

CHAPTER XVII

THE day wore on and, when the three did not come back with more fire, the crescent that had been squatting before the front door of the cottage moved away a little into the marshes, as though they were trying to look for them, or for some purpose we could not guess; and the men went out of the backdoor and also looked over the marshes, but in the opposite direction, looking to see if any more of their comrades were coming. Men and monsters were both disappointed. Then, seeing us moving about, the monsters came back, and we all had to get into the little house again. Round they came then and watched by the backdoor, as well as the front one and under the window, and it was obvious that they were waiting for an adequate supply of fire with which to burn the house. All day we waited, and they did not come back with the fire. I never knew a longer day. In the afternoon, through a hole in the backdoor a policeman on watch saw three more motors coming out from the edge of the town, and there were police in all of them. This time they had rifles, and what looked like machine-guns. The man reported it to the inspector, and Pender said at once: "Tell them to keep away. Rifles will be no use."

So the inspector signalled out of the window with a flag that he made from a towel tied on to a piece of wood. He did not signal as they signal in the Army and Navy, because he would have had to have leaned out of the window for that, and the monsters underneath would have reached up and caught him; but he pushed it out of the window and withdrew it, leaving it a second or two for a dash and pulling it back instantly for a dot. To show them his method of signalling quickly he signalled first S O S, three shorts, three longs and three shorts, knowing that they would pick up that quicker than anything else. But, having asked for help, he told them next to keep away and that their rifles were no use, and then he followed Ablard Pender's suggestion and asked for artillery.

"We are all right now," said Pender to me, "if they come in time. I've got him to believe me. It's all right now that they are taking it seriously. Once they do that, these things can't beat the whole armed force of the country. But they can if people don't take it seriously. It's as serious as any revolution that there has ever been, unless they take it in time."

"Well, he has asked them to," I said.

"Yes," said Pender. "But I hope they'll hurry."

And he looked out of the window over the marshes in the direction in which the three had gone. Still there was no sign of smoke. We learnt during that signalling that the inspector's name was Inspector Crabble. We asked him rather anxiously what answer the others had given, for they had turned and gone away.

"They were trying to get through on a walkie-talkie," he said. "But we could only hear atmospherics. Then they got out a handkerchief and signalled."

"What did they signal?" I asked.

"They said O.K.," said Inspector Crabble.

"I hope the guns will arrive in time," said Pender.

"They'll come as quick as they can," said the inspector, "if the War Office send them."

"But they must send them," said Pender. "Our civilization is at stake." And, turning to me, he said: "Do help me explain, so that they must understand."

But I could not explain. For what is our civilization? It is something as intricately connected with machinery as an

American cotton-plantation was once connected with slavery. To remove machinery from our civilization now would be an uprooting that would result in the starvation of millions. So what we had to defend against the machine was something of which the machine was a very large part. Only, this grim worker was now becoming the master, and must be thrust back to its place. I could not explain now, and left it to Pender. "After all, you started it," I said.

We had now eaten the last food in the house, and had only tea left, which may have made us irritable, or the long strain of danger may have irritated Pender; for he replied: sharply: "I told you I never started it. It's been going on steadily for more than a hundred and fifty years. I only had a part in it, as we all had. Yes, all of us. Not everybody improved the inventions we had as I did; but anyone that ever went in a train or a motor-bus, or went up in a lift or turned on an electric light acquiesced in them. Yes, all acquiesced; and you have no right to say what you did."

"I am sorry," I said.

And at that moment Alicia came up.

"We are all sorry, Ablard," she said. "But don't let's worry about it now. Don't you see all those faggots that they have got against the doors and the window? They have only got to come back and light them. Don't you see that they can burn us all, and that we can't stop them? So don't worry about things now. They are all of the past, and that's gone. We've only got the present, and not much of it."

After that we all spoke more freely, seeing that we need not worry about Alicia, who saw the whole situation clearly enough. Though one thing I was able to point out to her, which was that, if the War Office sent the artillery, it could come very quickly, from perhaps no farther than Woolwich, which was quite close; whereas the monsters were now moving appreciably slower, like old men of the fens with rheumatism settling down in their joints.

The day wore away, and neither the artillery came nor the three monsters with fire. Sometimes an arm came through one of the holes in the door, and groped about and withdrew. And once a pair of those steel claws rapped against each pane of the window and broke it, and slid in and clutched at the man who was watching, and missed him. Then it waved about and slowly withdrew, and Eerith followed it up with one of his basins of water.

Alicia went back to look after the wounded man, who seemed to be delirious now; for he was talking of beetles that had mated with tigers, and saying that their cubs were pursuing him. Watching for those iron arms to come through the doors and wave like tendrils of creepers in a wind and clutch like claws of lobsters, none of us thought of the weather, or noticed that a louring sky was hanging grey on the marshes. But now Eerith, who had not been looking out of the window, gave a shout.

"What?" I said.

"Rain," exclaimed Eerith, pointing to where a few drops had hit what was left of the broken panes. "They don't like wet more than cats. It will keep them away for a bit, the ones that have gone for the fire. It won't burn either."

"That must have been why the others have not got back already," said Pender. "They would have been watching the sky and are sheltering."

"Could they do that?" asked Inspector Crabble.

"I've told you," said Pender. "They are more intelligent than we. If we don't realize that, we shall be making a bad mistake, of which they will be sure to take advantage."

"But can they see?" he asked.

"The one that I made can," he said.

"And is that one of the ones that went away for more fire?" the inspector asked.

"No," said Pender. "I think that one's here. They all look much alike. It made the rest like itself. But I think it's here."

"But the others can't see, can they?" I said.

"I'm afraid it can see for all of them," answered Pender. "I'm afraid it can do what the queen termite-ant can do."

"But how?" I asked.

"I've no idea," replied Pender.

"But you made it," I said.

"Good lord," said Pender. "How many men know what the things they have made are going to do? How many men know anything really of the personalities of their own sons, or how they came by them? Do you suppose that James Watt had any idea of what England would look like a hundred and fifty years after he was dead? Do you think he would not have felt lost in a factory city? Do you think that Marconi foresaw Mussolini or Hitler?"

"But wait a moment," I said. "I didn't mean to annoy you. What had Mussolini or Hitler to do with Marconi?"

"Only that he made them," said Pender. "Do you think they could ever have got where they did without wireless? Gladstone's Midlothian campaign was held up as a wonder. Night after night he addressed meetings all through the autumn. How many people do you suppose heard him in that record campaign? Two thousand a night, do you suppose? As many as eighty nights? A hundred and sixty thousand men. And it was a record, mind you. How many did Hitler speak to, do you suppose, in an hour? Whenever I have heard him screaming, a hundred million others must have heard him at the same time. Can't you see that he was one of the beasts that Marconi made? And now you're blaming me."

"I'm not blaming you," I said.

"No, we're not blaming you," said the inspector soothingly.

"No, but you're expecting me to know what things that I made are going to do," said Pender. "And I'm only telling you both that nobody ever did. How can they? You give things certain powers. But you don't know how they're going to use them. I don't even know how the queen termite-ant works. I only know that along those wires that I made, certain currents run in the same way. What the brain of that ant can do, those wires can do, and we've got to recognize it. We think ourselves pretty intelligent. The only reasoning creatures, we used to say. Is it wonderful that we can invent something as good as the brain of an ant? It oughtn't to seem too wonderful to us, considering what we thought of ourselves. Unless I can get you to understand that, and that you must stop this revolution now, you will never stop it."

"All right, sir, all right," said the inspector, to whom Pender turned as he said the last sentence, almost shouting it into his face. "It's all right. We have sent for the artillery."

"Well, I am glad you have," said Pender a little mollified. "Because if they get in here and get the oil that they want, to keep themselves as agile as ever, they'll influence all machines. You saw what they did to your motors and to those other motors and to your walkie-talkie. All that will spread. They'll control everything mechanical in the earth or the ether. And our day will be over."

"How many of them are there?" asked Inspector Crabble.

"Twenty or thirty, I should say," said Pender.

"And can that number do what you seem to be afraid of?" he asked.

"They can make more, you see," said Pender. "There might very soon be forty of them."

"Could forty do it?" Inspector Crabble asked.

"Fewer than that have done it," said Pender.

"Done what?" asked the inspector.

"Overthrown empires," said Pender. "Shattered old regimes and then slaughtered whomever they liked. These will be the headquarters of it. What some people might call a kind of *politburo*. They will influence all the rest. I don't know how. You've seen the beginning of it. The end of it will be the end of everything. Or what we call everything. I suppose the world will go on, but our day will be over."

"We can't go out like that," I said.

And the inspector merely smiled.

"Can't we!" said Pender. "Have you ever studied geology?"

"I can't say I have," I answered.

"Well," said Pender, "I've seen a cliff full of fossils, and near the top of it a layer of oyster shells more than a foot deep running for miles. For hundreds and hundreds of years there must have been nothing but oysters living there. They couldn't have imagined any other life, except an occasional fish. And then above them came a layer of flints. Some disaster had overtaken every oyster. Not one left. We should go out like that. Or be kept as slaves."

And then Alicia came up with a cup of tea and gave it to Pender. And he thanked Alicia and drank the tea, and became calmer. "I may have been a little excited," he said then. "I think you would be every bit as excited as I, if you could see as clearly as I do what is coming."

"I'm sure we should," said Inspector Crabble.

"It's been coming nearer for years," said Pender. "And now——"

But whatever he was going to say was interrupted by a shout from the policeman who was watching through one of the holes in the front door. "They are moving," he said.

And at the same moment this same report came from the backdoor and the window. The things were all moving together, as though by one impulse.

"What are they doing?" I asked.

"I don't know," said Pender.

All the police became very alert. We could see the things moving away from the window and round the house, and we heard them clattering away from the backdoor and from the front door, coming towards each other. When they met they stopped, and the ones from under our window joined them on the opposite side of the house, where there was neither window nor door, and we heard their metallic bumps against that wall. We heard a creaking about their legs as they moved, which we had not heard before. But now all sound had stopped; the last one had bumped its iron body against the wall, and they were now crouched there in silence.

"What are they doing?" I asked again.

And a policeman went into the bedroom in which the

I

sick man lay, and called to another to assist him; and we heard them moving a chest-of-drawers and a chair, and heard the skylight opened, and then a pause.

"What are they doing?" asked the inspector.

And then there came the answer from the next room: "They are sheltering from the rain, sir."

The inspector went into the bedroom and came back.

"That's what they are doing," he said. "They are sheltering against the wall on the leeward side of the house, under the edge of the thatch."

"Can they get shelter there?" I asked Eerith.

"Oh yes, sir," he said, "they can, till the thatch begins to drip. The wind is against this window. Like cats they are. I used to slip out of the backdoor sometimes and souse them, when they were caterwauling round the house. The cats, I mean. I'll do it now."

And he got his basin and went to the backdoor. Very slowly he opened it, and stole out with the quiet step of one that was accustomed to deal with tom cats as he said. Just as he threw the water the chief one saw him, and all of them turned their heads towards Eerith as smartly as a platoon obeying an order, and several of them creaked as they did it. He threw the water along a row of their backs, and dashed round the corner of the house and in at his backdoor as they all rushed at him. That sudden turn of their heads I did not see; but Eerith told me of it, and their rush at him I certainly heard. It was like a mass of machinery starting all at once. Eerith got in safely and locked the door. We were standing anxiously by it to see him get in.

"You can't do that again," I said.

"No," Eerith said. "They'll be watching. But I soaked most of them. I can get the rest from the skylight."

We heard the monsters lumbering back to the wall under which they were sheltering, and the rain became heavier.

"That will keep the others away," he said.

Eerith struck me as knowing more about those monsters than even Pender did.

"They be sheltering over there beyond the marshes," he said, "somewhere on the dry land, wherever they got their fire from. But I'll give these a bit more water."

And he went into the bedroom where Alicia was looking after the sick man, and we heard him climb on to the chest-of-drawers that two of the policemen had put under the skylight. And I think that he had a chair on top of that. He must have opened the skylight too softly for us to hear him. Then he gave a low whistle, and must have signed to a man who stood in the doorway to bring his basin of water, for he filled the basin and carried it into the room.

"Is all this very good for the sick man in the bedroom?" asked the inspector.

And Pender said: "If only you would realize that the fate of mankind is at stake, you would not ask things like that. If Eerith can do anything to annoy them before the artillery comes up, it is all to the good. And they don't seem to like water. Never leave the enemy alone to plan at his ease, whoever he is."

"Can water do all that?" the inspector asked.

"They don't seem to like it," said Pender.

Suddenly we heard a commotion and a clatter of iron against the opposite wall from our window, and they had evidently had another shower of water from the basin with which Eerith used to throw it over the cats.

We looked at the sky and wondered how long the rain would last. For certainly, if the others sheltered from it like this, the three would not venture through it over the marshes, especially when they wanted to carry burning logs. And we felt safe for a while, though it was not of our safety that we should have been thinking, but of that of mankind. For if they broke into the cottage and got the oil that they wanted before it burned, that dreadful committee would be able to exert its influence from there; and the workers of the world, the workers that had never done anything else but work, the heartless and soulless machines, would sweep the drones away, as we must seem to them, or make slaves of us, and dominate the world as we have done in our time, and many great beasts before us.

Again there came a clatter and rattle of wrathful machinery, as another basin of water went down from the skylight.

CHAPTER XVIII

"THEY'LL go soon, like those tom cats," shouted Eerith from his perch under the skylight.

And we heard continuous rattling outside the walls from uneasy joints of machinery. One more splash from the basin and they were off, and past the front of the house, and I could see them come in sight from the window all moving together, but not so fast as they used to. They went barely a hundred yards, and then they stopped where a cluster of bulrush leaves was growing, and turned their heads to the house.

"Any chance, do you think?" I asked the inspector.

"No," he said. "I don't think we can go fast enough. And there's the sick man and the lady."

"If you mean running as far as the town," said Pender, "we couldn't do it. They are only a hundred yards away, and it isn't long enough start. And besides, they may want us to do it. It is very likely a trap."

But then we saw what they were doing among the bulrushes. They were picking the broad leaves with their sharp nippers and holding them over that vulnerable joint where what I have called the head joined on to what looked like the body, and would have been body, had they been beetles. But what Pender had made was really only a brain, with legs and a bundle of arms, and great iron plates to protect that devilish brain. In the front part, that moved and seemed to watch one, so like the head of a beetle, were the delicate ears and, in the monster he made, eyes, whose vision was only limited by the hills. These eyes it had only been able to imitate with pieces of steel cut into minute facets, whose vision must have been dim. Evidently they feared the rain less than Eerith's basins of water, though they feared the rain too, for they had been so carefully sheltering from it; and now they were cutting these broad leaves of the bulrushes and waving them in the air to dry them, and putting them over the joint that seemed to correspond to our necks.

"What are they doing now?" asked Inspector Crabble.

"Wrapping their heads up to keep out the rain," said Pender.

"Can they do that?" he asked.

"Elephants can do that much," said Pender. "Once when a zoo was bombed, an elephant ran into a neighbouring pool and crouched in the water and broke a branch off a tree with his trunk, and put it over his back to hide himself. Elephants are less intelligent than Man, or so we believe. I tell you again that these things are more intelligent than what we are. We must understand that they can do at least what an elephant can, or we shall never be able to deal with them."

"Yes, I see," said Inspector Crabble, looking out of the window. "They are holding the leaves on their backs with some of what you call their hands. Yes, I see that they can."

In an ominous crescent they crouched there, watching the house. And the rain still drizzled on.

"Scatter the logs away from the wall," said the inspector to some of his men, "so that they will get the most of the rain."

And two or three men ran out from each of the doors and pushed the logs farther away. And we could see the line of monsters turning their heads and intently watching them. But none of them made a rush, and the men came back into the house and locked the doors again. I did not see very much use in what they had done, because the three that had gone away to the dry land out of our sight could bring plenty of dry logs back, as well as more straw, and once they got that alight they would be easily able to burn wet logs and all.

"Hadn't you better pour your drums of oil away," said the inspector to Eerith, "if they are so keen on it?"

Eerith thought for a moment, and then he said: "Some would lie on the ground in puddles and a lot of it would run down to the water and float, and they would gather some of it up."

"That's right," said Pender. "Don't let them have any."

And so we kept the oil in the house. That room in the little cottage was heavy with cigarette smoke, for the policemen had plenty of cigarettes with them. And some of them strolled out of the backdoor to get some fresh air. But this brought the monsters nearer, and their crescent closed slowly in to within a few yards of the cottage. All the men got back in time.

"How did they know that the men had just gone out?" I asked Pender. "They couldn't have seen the backdoor from where they were."

"I am afraid it's those ears," said Pender. "We mustn't assume that there is anything that they cannot hear anywhere."

"What a wonderful thing you have made, Pender," I said, and couldn't help adding the word, "unfortunately."

"Not a bit more wonderful than the cheapest wireless set," said Pender. "Only we have got used to them. Tell my story to the ghost of your grandfather and tell him all that you can about wireless sets, and he'll simply refuse to allow that either story is in the least credible. I don't think those ears that I made can hear anything much more than a few miles away; but a wireless set can hear words said in New York, and some can reply to them. We live amongst wonders."

"Yes, I suppose so," I said.

"The only unfortunate thing," he continued, "is that we who controlled our wonders can do so no longer."

Then the sight of Alicia coming through the bedroom door and returning with a cup of tea reminded me of the sick man. Sometimes I could not help feeling that to forget him, as some of us did while trying to guess the next move of the monsters, was callous, and sometimes it seemed silly to think of him at all while such a peril menaced mankind. I am afraid Pender thought nothing of him, and sometimes I thought that perhaps he forgot mankind, with the exception of one of its members, who was Alicia.

Birds in a bush of lilac in Eerith's garden, the only perch for them as far as the eye could see, began to sing in the rain.

The long deep gashes that the monster had made in the man it had seized were now less inflamed, and Alicia said that he no longer spoke rapidly of incomprehensible things, and that his pulse was getting down towards a hundred, and that he sometimes slept.

Eerith had found a tin of biscuits, which promised us a cheerless supper of one biscuit each, and one each for breakfast next day; and after that no more, though the tea was still holding out. The milk was kept for the sick man, with a good deal of sugar to mitigate the taste of the milk, for it had turned. The rest of us drank tea without any milk, as one does in times of stress. And how good it tastes! But we forget that, when milk is again available, and we pour it once more into our tea.

The birds sang on in the lilac, the rain continued to fall, and the wind went over the marshes like a horse that the rain was riding, lightly trampling the rushes, and the monsters continued to watch. Cigarettes were now giving out as well as the food, and there was no sign of help coming; the greyness of sky and marshes blended in one bleakness, and the men began to sing. One of them raised his voice in some song of a county I did not know, telling small things of life among farmlands and woods, such as men live no longer now: even some of the phrases were obsolete. But the rest joined in and sang, as though the things of which they told were as real to them as they had been once to their grandfathers. I always remember that scene, because the rain and the monsters and the lack of food and the absence of any help, and our inability to call for any by wireless, and the stuffy air in the crowded room, with many lesser things, had about then combined to bring our cheerfulness to its lowest; and at that moment they sang. And from the bedroom the sick man joined in. Almost as though the wind heard it, as it seemed to our fancies, wakened up by the song, a blue band appeared in that part of the sky from which the rain had been coming. Upward it spread and towards us; and when the song was ended, so was the rain. We had nothing but good from the rain, and yet the impressions that our minds receive are not received from logic, and we were all cheered by the lifting of the rain. Not that we saw at once that it had lifted, for the beds of tiny rivulets that time had worn in the thatch had now their runnels of water, and one of them dripped past our window long after the rain was over.

As the light began to dim with the coming of evening the monsters came in closer and closer, and were soon round both doors again, and some were watching a little way off from the window.

And now, cast down from the sky, colours appeared in the marshes like those that flicker in opals. And then above their pale beauty, like one black wing, went a flight of starlings, and disappeared like a sigh lost in the evening. A line of singing birds next, dipping up and down in their flight, also went home, to what trees I could not tell, for none were in sight. And then, their voices solemn above the songbirds' twitter, high in the lucid vault which evening seemed to have cut from a pale beryl, the rooks went slowly over and passed out of sight and hearing. Silence came then and night hovered; and, just between day and night, green plover wailed over the waste, and went away to the distance like lamentable lost spirits. What would happen to birds, I wondered, if machines should get hold of the world? If they enslaved men, what would they do to birds? And then I began wondering if we had treated the birds well, or if we abused our power while we had it. I thought about this for a long time, because much seemed to depend on it. If we were worthy to hold the world I believed we would hold it still; but if not, I feared that we might lose our hold some day, and this menace that faced us now might be the one to dethrone us. I did not think so much of the birds that we kill for our food: we were no worse than the tiger there. But I thought long about cages. And while I was immersed in these mournful thoughts the Evening Star appeared, and the sight of its silver beauty set in the pale turquoise of the western sky, somehow cheered me and I could not think that machines that have no sense of beauty could prevail in the end over us who through that sense divine the unity of all nature. For, though we deny it sometimes, and sometimes desecrate beauty, that sense is in all of us. I had seen the work of machines and could not believe that, however brilliant Pender's invention was, however far its intellect might transcend ours, there could be a sense of beauty in the core of any machine. I gazed at the Evening Star and felt some link uniting mankind with the rest of creation, and felt that upon creation machines intruded, and trusted that, however dreadful their power, yet by means that I could not see they would be prevented from extending over the earth the revolution now raging around us.

CHAPTER XIX

WHILE distant windows still shone rather with colour than light, vying in beauty with flowers, there twinkled from where the town ran down to the marshes the light of an electric torch sending a signal, and, as soon as it was seen from our window, Inspector Crabble drew a torch from his pocket and answered. And then the message came. It was to say that the War Office had replied to the request of the police, and that a battery of artillery had been sent and would be here in half an hour. We looked over the marshes in the

direction in which we expected the three monsters with the
burning logs, that they would now be able to carry, and saw
no sign of fire there, and felt for the first time that we had a
reasonable chance. You would have thought that at this
good news the policemen would have sung again, but everyone became very silent. From the signalling flashes the
monsters round the house were intelligent enough to know
that something was to be expected from the direction in
which a few distant windows were glowing, and in the light
that Inspector Crabble threw on them now and then from
his torch we saw they had turned their heads and seemed
to be watching; but not in the direction in which we were
looking for any sign of the artillery, but away over the
marshes towards the point from which they expected their
own reinforcements. From this we knew that the ones which
had gone for the fire must be coming; for, with their strange
power of thinking all together, which wireless is increasingly
giving to us, there could be no doubt that they knew what
the others were doing. We therefore gazed in the same direction, and several of us looked at our watches. One by one we
looked again, and then held them up to our ears. All of the
watches were wrong by several hours. I set my watch to
what I guessed was the time, when about a quarter of an
hour had gone by since we heard about the artillery. But,
though I got the hands to about the right time, they would
not stay there and started to move rapidly backwards. And
shortly after the inspector had first turned the light on the
monsters from his electric torch, its mechanism went out of
order. The light in our little room came from candles, on
which nothing the monsters could do had any effect. Alicia
wore a gold wrist-watch, and I went to the door of the bedroom where she was sitting by the sick man and asked her if
she could tell me the time, hoping that her watch, which
was better than any of ours, might be unaffected. She raised
her wrist to look, and an expression of utter astonishment
covered her face. Without a word she lifted her wrist towards
me, and I saw that the hands were spinning round as fast

as the eye could follow. From astonishment her mood gave place gradually to tears. And so Pender found her, as he came to the door of the room in which she was.

"Oh, Ablard," she said. "Look!"

It was as though at that moment she saw the strength of the enemy, and perhaps even feared defeat. So doleful she seemed in that moment, that she may have looked even further than defeat and seen the terrible fate in store for the world, when we were gone from our proud position like old things lost in deep strata, and Earth's master would be the machine. I went back to the main room as Ablard Pender came up to her, but I heard him say as I left: "Don't be sad, Alicia. The artillery are just coming up."

"Oh, look what they can do, Ablard," I heard her say, holding up her spinning watch to him.

"I think it's only local," he said consolingly. "I think the clocks in London are still obeying us. The artillery will stop them."

But I could not hear or see any sign of artillery. Still I heard Pender's voice trying to console Alicia. And then, clear from the next room, I heard the voice of the sick man saying: "Don't worry, miss. The police have the situation well in hand."

And when I heard him say that, and thought of our plight, that our food had given out and the monsters surrounded us, and all machines seemed obeying them, and not a gun had come, I knew that, in spite of Alicia's care, his delirium was returning.

I went to our broken window and looked towards the town, but saw no sign of movement. The monsters were lying round the window still, and far windows glowed in the direction in which we vainly hoped for artillery. I had seen by day the houses from which those lights now glowed, and seen them without interest; but only their exteriors showed then. Now the glow that cheered the night from so many windows came from the hearts of the houses, and showed that the lonely night was filled with homes. Now it was quite dark in the night overhead, and the glare of London lit the lower parts of the sky: still high above it the Great Bear went on his long prowl, with neck and nose stretched out, sniffing towards Boötes. How unconcerned the constellations appeared with the fate of Man, which seemed to depend so much on whether we should be starved out in this insignificant cottage and these enemies of mankind be able to obtain the oil that they needed before the promised artillery came. The calm stars helped me to think. I realized now, that machines had always been our enemy: they had served us because they had to, not because there was anything in their nature that was in the least attuned to ours. So far as there could be sensation in those old crude machines before Pender perfected his monster, they hated us. I could see that now. One only had to look, had one ever thought of it, at anything Man made with his hands, with his wandering fancies chiselled or carved all over it, and compare that with the cold grim heartless shape of the things the machine made. It was clear enough, looking back on it: the machine was a sullen slave. How long was it likely to serve us? Just as long as it was unable to tear us to pieces, as Pender's monster had torn that dog. But now through the work of Pender the machine had got the power to fight with Man and was doing so; and, looking at all we could see of it, which was not far, the machine appeared to be winning.

It would have come in any case. It was very near that point, when Pender started upon his fatal work. Machines were improving every year, and some man's work would have done it. Indeed machines were already far stronger than Man. They only needed that subtlety called intelligence, which after all is no subtler than any wireless set, or the mechanism of the anti-aircraft shell that bursts when it feels it is near enough to the aeroplane. That slight extra subtlety Pender had given to the machine and, now that it could use its mighty power intelligently, it naturally used it against us. I believed Pender when he told me that the influence of those monsters reached only a few miles. I knew that the siege of a cottage among the marshes was only a small affair; but I knew that all revolutions were small affairs at the outset, and prospered if not stopped immediately. And I looked towards the town again and saw no lights moving nor heard any hum of the motors that would bring the guns. Then I looked in the other direction, to which, as far as I could see of their black shapes in the dark, the monsters besieging our window were watching. Still I saw no light of any approaching fire. But there seemed an air of expectancy among the things in front of the window, that made me feel that the others were surely coming.

I asked the inspector, then, if he thought we should get the artillery.

"Oh yes," he said. "The War Office promised it. It is sure to be coming soon."

"What about signalling again?" I asked.

"We might do it with a candle," he said.

And from his readiness to adopt my suggestion, I realized that he was more uneasy than he had let me see hitherto. He put the candle out of the window, partly sheltering it with his cap, which also concealed its light from the town. Then he lowered the cap and raised it with long or short intervals. The wick was long and the candle luckily stayed alight, and so Inspector Crabble signalled with the Morse code, asking when the artillery was coming. The message was picked up and answered, and the answer was 'Coming soon'.

For the next five or ten minutes we did little but watch in both directions, to our left to the edge of the town, and to our right to that part of the marshes from which we expected the three to come with fire, wondering which of the two would come first. We had no longer anything left in the fire-extinguisher, and the wet from the rain must have been drying in the night air from the store of logs that the monsters had laid against our two doors and under the window. A flush appeared in the sky, as if the moon were rising in a part of it that we could not see from our window, a waning moon that did nothing to dim the stars. And then we saw the light of a lantern signalling from the edge of the town. They were no longer using an electric torch. The message said that owing to a technical hitch in one of the motors propelling the guns, the battery could not arrive in time that night, but that a battery of Territorial trench mortars would do the work quite as well, and would arrive during the morning. The inspector made no comment upon this message; but I asked him why, if one of the motors had broken down, the remaining five guns did not come, or at any rate three, if it was a four-gun battery.

"Well," said the inspector, "a battery likes to work all together." But I saw from the insufficiency of his answer that he knew that all the self-propelled guns must have broken down as soon as they had entered the area that was under the influence of these devilish things. Even, for all I knew, they might have turned against their gunners. And immediately after that message we saw three blazing lights moving over the marshes from the direction in which the three monsters had gone. There was a stir among the black shapes watching our window, and a kind of purring arose from them which I had not heard before, and a certain alertness among them seemed to show that they had a confidence which none of us in the cottage had any longer. I called to Pender, who was in the small room with Alicia, and he came to where we were standing by the window.

"They are coming," I said to Pender. And from the tone of my voice he knew which lot I meant.

"Well, we beat them off last time," he said.

"We have no fire-extinguishers left," I said, "and not much water. And they are bringing a lot more faggots."

I spoke in a low voice so that Alicia and the sick man should not hear. And then we looked over the marshes and saw the glow of burning logs coming nearer, and the reflections of them flaming in the water on each side of the monsters that carried them. Loud bumps against our front door told us that the monsters there were rearranging and piling up their logs against it. It seemed to me that, if we could not hold out for the night, the revolution would have that lucky start that other revolutions have had, and that this one would be the last; that this one would take the supremacy from mankind, and none of us would recover it. A mournful thought perhaps, but men sometimes have mournful thoughts when a few of them are alone in the night with an enemy that is completely their superior, and with no hope of any help for a long time.

"How will the trench mortars come?" I asked Inspector Crabble.

"Oh, they will come in the usual way," he said.

"But supposing their mortars go on strike like the rest?" I asked.

"Well, if those things can really do that," said the inspector, "they can put the mortars in farm carts."

"It will make a delay," I said.

"Yes," he replied, "but they'll get them here all right."

And I could see no way in which the monsters could stop them doing that.

"At what range do you think they will engage them." I asked.

"Probably about four hundred yards," said the inspector. "They will blow them all to pieces all right."

Meanwhile the monsters with the logs were coming nearer across the marshes.

"Most of them are all round the cottage," I said. "How shall we get out of the way of the trench mortars?"

"We probably shan't have to," said the inspector. "They'll probably attack the trench mortars when they come. They seem to attack everything."

"If they come with horses and carts," said Pender, "they are bound to attack. They are sure to hate horses."

"The trench mortars will catch them all as they come towards them," said Crabble.

"Why do they hate horses?" I asked Pender.

"Part of the old regime," he said. "They hate them as Lenin or Trotsky would have hated a lady. Horses are part of the old way, the old way in which the world had been going on for ever. I know, because I thought that I could improve on it. Horses were so slow and ineffectual. I know well enough what that thing I made thinks of them. They'll attack horses."

"And if they don't?" I asked.

"If they don't," he said, "the trench mortars will come nearer until they do. Don't you think so, Inspector? And, if they still don't attack, we'll have to make a bolt for it and try to reach the soldiers."

Those were the plans we made; but they concerned some time next day, and now it was night and the three bundles of flaming logs came nearer. Pender glanced towards them and I could see he despaired, and he went back to talk to Alicia. I did not hear what he said to her. But I heard the sick man repeat: "We have it well in hand."

"How much water have we left?" I asked Eerith.

"Very little, sir," he said.

"What shall we do?" I asked.

The inspector said nothing. But Eerith answered: "If only I could get my old gun I could have a crack at them. I can see it lying there, and none of them things are near it."

At that moment Pender rejoined us. "Your gun is no good against them," he said.

"Still I should like to get it," he said. "I don't like to see it lying there covered with rust."

I don't know when a gleam of hope came to my mind, but I think it was then as I heard Eerith say the word rust.

CHAPTER XX

WHILE we were in that house surrounded by monsters I wondered again and again what Mrs. Ingle was doing, and Alicia's mother and Eliza. Afterwards I often talked to all three of them, and from those talks I pieced this story together. What they all seem to have done, from the time that Ablard Pender left them and for all the rest of the day, was to worry; to wonder, that is to say, when he was coming back, and what had happened to him and to Alicia, and when they would hear of it, and a great many more things than I am able to guess. For nobody can keep pace with a mind that is worrying. All that day they worried and probably all the night; and early next morning when Ablard had not returned and there was no news of Alicia, Mrs. Ingle decided that the worst possible things had all occurred, and had persuaded Mrs. Maidston to agree with her. Only the good sense of Eliza saw any hope, out of which she gave ample unheeded consolation. Mrs. Ingle had telephoned a great deal to the police during the day, as well as during the night. I don't know what she said to them. But I do know that late that night, and for the rest of the night, whenever she rang up the police, she got the answer: "Number engaged." Before the police lost their patience with her, as I imagine they did, they told her enough, whatever they said, to give her the idea that the place to which to go for the information she naturally wanted was those marshes beside the Thames in which Pender had allowed his monster to do its dangerous work.

I cannot quite analyse Mrs. Ingle's feelings. I think that Mrs. Maidston had in some way mysterious to me conveyed all her own anxieties to her, so that Mrs. Ingle, however little she had at first welcomed Alicia to take over her nephew and Sandyheath from her, would now have made the telephone wires tremble, if she could, with her fears for Alicia. Her affection for Ablard Pender was probably the affection that she had had for him as a child, which lingered on into years when she had not entirely noticed that he had grown up, as she might have done had he become a chartered accountant at the age at which his father had done so. I believe that she thought of him as a child still, and knowledge that he had done something affecting the fate of mankind, which had so dazzled her brain, had not perman-

K

ently altered her feelings towards him. And so she set out to find the greatest inventor, so far, of our age, very much in the spirit of one who looked for a lost child. She set out with Mrs. Maidston and Eliza to catch the very first bus that would take them to London through that bright morning.

London when they arrived had the alert look of a sleeper lying in the sun, about to awake. Many blinds were still down, and there were few in the streets, but those that walked in them seemed active and purposeful. Such was the impression of it that the three women seemed to have formed with their nerves all strung up by anxiety, and it may have been a foolish impression; but I am inclined to think that highly strung nerves see with a clarity denied to calmer minds and that, when their vision differs from the vision of dull content, it is theirs that is the truer. They went on to the starting place of the bus that should take them eastward, London waking about them noisily all the way.

Very few others were in that bus when they found it. Even on the face of the bus conductor, Eliza fancied she saw a faint surprise that anyone should be leaving London at that hour, when a million were trickling into it. He seemed to Eliza to sell them their tickets only because it was his duty and he meant to do it. But Eliza's nerves were all on edge and she was probably too fanciful. More clearly than either of the other women she saw what awaited them in the marshes.

Whether grudgingly, as Eliza fancied, or not, as we may more reasonably suppose, the bus turned away from the centre of London; and all the while those three women were wondering what had happened to Alicia and Ablard Pender. What they wondered they did not tell me, but into their wondering, and among the accidents that they imagined, there came from the real world the noise of a change in the note of the engines of their bus. They had grown so used to the noise of the engine, that it was completely part of their surroundings, and for long they had ceased to notice it. Now they noticed it: that was all. The bus continued its journey, with the slightly changed note. It was as noticeable as though you walked with a friend and his voice suddenly changed, or his character. None of the three attached any significance to it with their reason. But from something deeper in their minds I think their forebodings came up, bringing new fear. Then the bus stopped, and the driver got down and examined his engine. Then they went on; but the note of the engine was never quite the same as what it had been in the city.

The houses were smaller now, and Eliza seemed to have expected that the street would be narrower, but it was as wide as ever. Small gardens appeared, and they sometimes saw the golden flash of laburnum. Still that new note from the engine seemed to hint of some change. The three women listened to that note, as they could not help listening, and it probably intruded among their fears. The driver of course listened too, for he soon got down and examined the engine again. To him that new note would have boded nothing that was troubling anything more than his bus, though the conductor was heard to say to him that engine trouble had been developing in other buses along that route lately. All the driver said to that was: "Time the company got some new engines." But everything they said increased the fears of the three women, though I don't think they yet worked out any definite connection between what was wrong with the bus and any grim revolution of machines against men. The bus went slower as they neared their destination, uttering metallic coughs, and the noise jarred on the worn nerves of Mrs. Maidston.

"Aren't we near that side street now?" she said to Mrs. Ingle. And they seem to have agreed that they were and that it might be better to walk, especially as the bus had now started to skid. So, when it arrived uncertainly at the next stopping place, they all got out and walked a few hundred yards, and came to that last street of the little suburban town that ended at an arch of yellow brick, through which it stared at the marshes. Down this street they walked, every moment expecting something strange and even dreadful, with the skidding bus behind them and those marshes before. But there was nothing dreadful in the street at all; only a strange hush. Strangeness there certainly was; for all doors were closed, and some shutters, and the street was quite empty. Mrs. Maidston, Mrs. Ingle and Eliza walked along it and still saw no one, till they came to the end of the street and were about to walk under the railway arch, when a policeman walked out from the far side of it and stopped them.

"No one allowed through here, mam," he said.

"But why not?" said Mrs. Ingle.

"Well, there's a motorist been exceeding the speed limit in the built-up area, and some of the force are just coming to arrest him," said the policeman.

"But where is he?" asked Mrs. Ingle.

"Over there," the policeman said, pointing out to the marshes.

"A motor-car in the marshes?" said Mrs. Ingle.

"Well, we are not sure if he is quite sober," said the policeman. "But that will be for the doctor to say, and I can't give any opinion about that."

"But I think there's a young lady lost about here," said Mrs. Maidston, "and we must go and see."

"That's all been gone into," said the policeman, "and an inspector is coming to see about that. The young lady will be quite all right."

Three to one though it was, the policeman had held them back and had soothed their fears by telling them every now and then that an inspector was very soon coming with several police, and that everything would be all right. I don't think they were very long by that arch of yellow brick, standing on pavement and surrounded by houses in the midst of the works of Man, looking out at wild untamed nature, where reeds and water lay, and far off the Thames rode through them like a monarch in a procession.

Then the police arrived in the three motors that I have mentioned, stopping under the arch for a moment while the inspector spoke to the policeman, then going confidently on to the marshes. They saw the three cars stop and heard the firing, but one of the last of the hedges that cultivation had raised hid from them the sight of the policeman being seized by the monster.

I gathered that they spent much of the morning asking questions of the policeman in the archway, until he told them, in self-defence, I should say, of a shop a little way up the street, where they would be given lunch if they asked for it. Thither they went. And I imagine their going lifted a considerable burden from the imagination of the policeman. For the situation was a very difficult one to comprehend, because the approach to it during that policeman's lifetime, and indeed during the whole existence of the police force, had been so gradual that no one had noticed it.

Often a leader of revolutionaries appears to have risen up in a week; but he has been plotting for years, and gradually getting hold of his murderous power. So it was, not with Pender's machine, for that was only recently made, but with machinery, which had for so long been insidiously ousting Man. The policeman who, like nearly all of us, had noticed nothing of this, understood little of the situation with which men were now confronted. And, even had he done so, information in the possession of the police was not the property of whatever members of the public might come to inquire for it. Therefore he used his imagination and, in doing so, was far kinder to the three women than the bare truth would have allowed him to be. Without knowing it, long experience had given him many of the qualities of a hospital nurse; and he soothed the nerves of the three women and sent them away to get some food. It was in the little shop of a greengrocer that they were able to get a meal, when they knocked at the door and said that the policeman had recommended them to ask for it there.

The door was locked and the shutters were up, but a man came to the door in answer to their knocks and let them in. He showed them into the parlour at the back of his shop, where he brought them plenty of fish; and, whether or not he had his own dinner with them, he was in the room while they had theirs, and they had asked him why his shop was shut on a weekday.

"It's the police," he said. "They want us to keep all our doors shut today."

"But why?" asked one of the ladies.

"To keep any oil that we may have from being stolen," he said.

"But who is going to steal it?" one of them asked.

"There's something in the marshes that is not quite right," he replied.

"But what?" asked Mrs. Ingle.

"I don't quite know," said the man, "but we are to look out for anything coming from the marshes."

"But what is in the marshes?" asked Mrs. Ingle. "We were told a man with a car, who had been exceeding the speed limit."

"It may be a man," said the greengrocer.

After that I gathered that Mrs. Ingle and Mrs. Maidston both of them asked questions designed to receive answers that could assure them that what they feared was not true. But Eliza sat perfectly silent. No information they got could have been accurate; for no one outside the marshes knew what was going on there. Yet all the information they got corroborated their fears. It is curious how all the rumours they got in that street, so very contradictory though they were, yet somehow combined at last to make one picture, a picture of something dreadful haunting the marshes, weird as anything in a poem by Edgar Allan Poe, but strayed from its proper place in pages of poetry enjoyed by a winter fire, and appearing real and horrible in the marshes and threatening every door. For they left the house of the greengrocer after their dinner and entered the empty street, and often saw doors unlocked for a little while and faces peering out from between a door's edge and the doorpost. And at such doors they would stop and ask if Alicia had been seen, and what news there was from the marshes. Of Alicia they heard nothing; of the marshes little that could be called news; rather rumours and brief remarks. Sometimes short sentences like: "There's lights in the marshes." And then again what the greengrocer had said: "It may be men," a remark whose dreadful uncertainty chilled Mrs. Ingle's blood. And the woman who said it shut her door again, and they could hear her lock it at once.

CHAPTER XXI

THAT afternoon the second lot of police came along the street in three cars. The impression that the three women had as they saw them was that the drivers were pulling hard at their steering-wheels, as though they found it hard to hold their cars to their course, in spite of which the front car skidded, and the inspector spoke to the driver and called out an order to those behind him and they stopped the three cars and all got out. The three women noticed that they had rifles. Mrs. Ingle ran up to the inspector and asked him about Alicia, and the inspector told her that she was quite near and that they were going to get her at once.

"What is happening?" asked Mrs. Ingle.

"It's just some people over there," said the inspector, "who are making a little trouble in the marshes."

"People?" said Mrs. Ingle.

"Motorists," said the inspector.

"Is the girl all right?" asked Mrs. Ingle.

"Yes," said the inspector. "She'll be in the cottage. They are making a little trouble. But we'll soon put a stop to it."

Then she asked about her nephew, and was told that he would be there too. And the police moved on to the railway arch, and through it to the edge of the marshes, where they must have seen the signals that stopped them. Nobody was about in the street except Mrs. Maidston, Mrs. Ingle and Eliza. The police had warned the others to stay indoors.

Why these three were out and about I was not told, and drew
my own conclusions, which were that the authority of the
police, weakened by the flow of Mrs. Ingle's questions,
ceased to exert itself sufficiently to ensure that she sheltered
in one of the houses or went away; and walking about on the
road near the railway arch the police saw them as they
returned from the marshes, having got the signal from the
cottage to keep away. There they heard definitely that
Alicia and Ablard Pender were in the cottage and, in answer
to further questions, were told that the inspector there with
them wanted the reinforcements to stay at the edge of the
town, so as to trap the men that were giving trouble, as soon
as they retreated. But, empty though the road was, there was
a row of houses on each side which were full of people,
listening and talking; and a rumour rose up from the street,
from sources no more to be traced than those from which on
evenings of autumn a ghost-like mist would arise, a rumour
of guns. Guns, said voices at doors; the guns were coming.
And when the rumour reached the three women from a
doorway briefly opened and closed again, Eliza spoke with
an air of sure knowledge. "That is the stuff to give them,"
she said.

When Mrs. Maidston heard the rumour she went up to
the inspector near the railway arch, to remind him that
there were people in the cottage, and to ask him if they
would be safe if the guns should start shelling. Not of course
a very sensible question, considering that there were twelve
policemen in that cottage besides her daughter. Nor had the
time yet arrived when the inspector would admit that any
guns were coming at all, and in answer to questions about
them only replied that that would be a matter for the War
Office, about which he could say nothing. It was later that a
policeman went along the street, knocking at each door and
saying to whomever opened it. "Best stay indoors for today.
And don't mind if you hear a certain amount of noise. That
will be a few guns coming to do a bit of artillery-practice over
the marshes."

And when it was found that the discretion of this warning was rather too strong a dose for the people of that street, the policeman changed it by saying that some people had been giving trouble in the marshes and might have to be dealt with by the military authorities. So that they were not to mind if they heard a few guns firing. "Car bandits or something of the sort," he added in explanation. "Those sort of people will be getting up to their tricks. But we shall soon put a stop to them, with the help of the military authorities."

But one woman who came to the door at the sound of the knocking of the policeman said in reply to his warning: "Guns? I like guns." And her face lighted up with the memory of some solace they once had brought her. By the door of a house past which she seems to have been roaming aimlessly with Mrs. Maidston, followed always by Eliza, Mrs. Ingle heard the policeman speak of people giving trouble in the marshes. But at that moment a boy who had escaped from some neighbouring house in which his mother had locked him in, and climbed the railway embankment and looked from the top of it, trespassing on the line, ran by to get home to his house before his absence should be discovered, and heard the policeman speak of these people.

"People," he shouted to the three women as he went by. "They aren't people. They are machines. I seen 'em."

Eliza nodded to him, knowing he spoke the truth.

"Tin crabs, I call 'em," shouted the boy, and was gone.

The policeman was trained to take no notice of what boys shouted, and by discipline to obey orders. So he went on delivering the message that he had been ordered to give, from house to house, and the boy ran in front of him, calling out his far more accurate information, which made the policeman's warning a little out of date.

Even rain did not drive the three anxious women into the shelter of any house beyond what doorways supplied, and the sun set on them still scavenging for whatever scraps of information they could pick up; and these scraps did much to soothe them, for the soothing of the population was much

more the *métier* of the police than giving away accurate
information on what was soon to become a military under-
taking. But when the time came for the guns to arrive, the
street was carefully cleared by the police, not even stray boys
being allowed to run about any more. And Mrs. Maidston,
Mrs. Ingle and Eliza were led back to the greengrocer's shop
in which they had had their lunch, and were persuaded to sit
down to supper, and the door was then locked. The greengrocer and his wife sat down with them to the meal, and
over plenty of cold mutton the greengrocer talked of what
was going on. Mars is a strange wanderer. Born perhaps in a
palace, and starting from palaces so many of his journeys,
he will appear, and very often quite unexpectedly, amongst
the humblest cottages; or he may be found peeping round
hayricks, sleeping in cornfields, and drinking at muddy
streams. Now in the neighbourhood of one little street, and
the marshes where so few went and the cottage of Samuel
Eerith, events were occurring which much concerned the
destiny of mankind, and the greengrocer discussed it with
much the understanding that a fly might have, alighting by
chance on the first page of the work of Gibbon, that he
walked on a volume of history.

"Yes," said the greengrocer, "I should never be surprised
at anything that might go on in those marshes. When I was
young I remember old people that used to tell stories of
will-o'-the-wisps. And I've heard men say that smuggling
used once to go on there too. And when I saw those fires
that we've been seeing away over there of late, I said:
'Something is going on there again.' Didn't I, Edna?"

"Oh yes, you did," said his wife.

"Well, it is," said the greengrocer. "We wouldn't have all
those police here if it wasn't. And guns are coming, they say.
It will seem like old times."

"There are too many cars about nowadays," said the
greengrocer's wife. "It gives bandits and people like that too
many opportunities."

"Yes," said the greengrocer, "and they take to it young."

For one moment his wife had got near to the heart of the matter, when she mentioned too many cars. It was too much machinery that had led on year after year to the dreadful invention of Ablard Pender and to what was happening now. But they got no nearer to the true situation over that supper, for Mrs. Ingle said nothing that would have inculpated her nephew; and, though Mrs. Maidston said that her daughter had been taken to the cottage in the marshes, she said nothing of the dreadful machine that Ablard Pender was now calling Robespierre, and Eliza set perfectly silent. Then came the rumour that the guns were not coming after all. For sounds went clearly along the empty street; and footsteps heard again, or a mere shout, easily started the rumour, and it turned out to be true. For presently there came the sound of a knock on a door far up the street, and on another door and another, and the sound of doors opening, and then a policeman's voice explaining that, owing to a technical hitch in one of the motors that ran the guns, the artillery was not coming. At about this time the greengrocer looked up at his clock that hung opposite to him on the wall, and remained for some while staring at it with his mouth open. The hands were moving slowly backwards. All turned to look where the greengrocer was looking, and in the silence Eliza said: "Ah, they'd do that."

And nobody asked her what she meant.

The greengrocer recovered his composure then and said: "Well, we must stop it doing that, if we can, and put it right."

And he looked at his watch, but put it back in his pocket with a dissatisfied air.

"I'll go and dial Tim," he said, and he went out of the room. Presently he came back, saying: "The telephone is not working."

"My watch has gone wrong too," said his wife.

"I've heard of magnetic storms doing odd things," said the greengrocer.

"They are odd all right," said Eliza.

It is not often that people on battlefields know what is

happening, though unrelated bits of information drift in fast. As the night wore on it became clear in the green-grocer's house, what might have been noticed before, that the trains were not running. Their thunder was so familiar that it was scarcely heard as it passed, and that household had not known that it rumbled by no more. Now, looking back on it, the greengrocer and his wife remembered that no trains had been going by for some hours, and they gradually came to see, what everyone else in that street was seeing, that machines were dutiful servants of men no longer. What was going on beyond there they could not know, and could only interpret it by their awaking fears. Some may not even have noticed that trains no longer roared over the bridge by which they lived, nor ever looked at the time. Some may have feared a breakdown of all machines. Some, looking accurately between extremes, may have known that the breakdowns affected only a limited area. But probably none of those who lived in that street ever thought of a revolution planned in those marshes against the old supremacy of man-kind.

It is not often that any preach openly might is right. More often, where might is, those that possess it show logical argument in support of their claim to right. Machines had had might for some time. Now, thanks to Pender, they had a brain more brilliant than any of ours, well capable of argu-ment that those that had for long done most of the work of mankind should rightfully have the place that their power could so easily give them. It was a long-delayed revolution.

The greengrocer and his wife, Mr. and Mrs. Cable, gave a room to the three women for the night, providing a bedstead and a sofa, and a mattress on the floor with which Eliza was quite satisfied, and plenty of blankets. This supplied the three of them with a retreat which gave them a certain sense of security, but they did not think of going to bed, nor did the greengrocer or his wife. That the world was much con-cerned with what was happening where the little town ran down to the edge of the marshes and ended in that street under the railway embankment they never supposed; but that a heightening tension had come to that street, and every house round about it and the railway embankment and the marshes beyond, they were well aware. Such heightenings of tensions are never missed, and never can be. Even when not spoken of, and they seldom are, they are conveyed by the glance of an eye or the expression of a face. It isn't necessary for people whose communal temperature is thus raised to know what the feeling of tension all round them is about, or the rights and wrongs of it or its ancient causes, but they feel it as lightning is felt, even before it strikes. And now people spoke to each other with more alertness, even if they spoke about trifles and not of the strange events that were occurring around them; and they seemed to see things, even things that were of no importance, with a quicker perception. And of course that quickened perception was not only of the eye: faint sounds were quickly picked up and, quickest of all, rumours. Probably many false ones ran down that street. But of those I did not hear.

Soon a rumour came that, on account of the technical hitch, trench mortars would be sent instead of artillery, in order to deal with the car bandits that had been giving trouble; and, where the embankment rose against the sky, the police were seen by the light in the west from the remnants of what remained of a summer's day, strengthening the wire paling that ran on each side of the railway. For some while policemen had been collecting whatever wire could be found in that neighbourhood; and rumour said, and rumour is not always wrong, especially when the story is told afterwards, that they were protecting against any possible attack the position that was to be taken up by the trench mortars.

Meanwhile all clocks were moving eccentrically, no watches showed the right time, no motors entered that street or were heard in the neighbourhood, no telephones worked, no wireless sets, no electric appliances in such houses as had them, no electric light, no machinery whatever, or, if it worked, it worked perversely, obeying

no man any more. All these events were local, confined
to a few miles. But how local are all the great battles of
history, until our day when we string them out across
continents; yet how far-reaching is their effect upon
mankind. All the people in that street, who were so near to
the centre of these affairs and were the first to feel anything
of this revolution, knew of it as much and no more than a
cottager on a battlefield knows of the destinies that are
burning his hayrick.

Then late at night in a room lighted by candles, that
the greengrocer fortunately had amongst his goods, he
and his wife and their three guests, and all the street,
heard ring through the stillness a sound they had nearly
forgotten, as down the road came farm-horses dragging
farm-carts.

CHAPTER XXII

IN the cottage in the marshes, that same night, we were
watching the glare of the flaming logs coming nearer, as the
three monsters approached us, casting over the water around
them long brilliant streaks such as sometimes are seen to
glow from a stormy sky. There was no fire-extinguisher left.

"How much water have you?" the inspector asked of
Samuel Eerith.

"Only enough for our drinking water now," said Eerith.

"Use it all to put out the fire when it comes," said the
inspector. "We shan't need any drinking water if we are
burned alive."

Eerith tried to plead for a little water to be kept back, if
only for tea. "We haven't enough to put out a fire, sir," he
said. "But it would make three or four pots of tea."

But Inspector Crabble put first things first, and would not
deviate from his order that all water must be used on the
fire.

"Are they coming any nearer?" he asked of one of his men at the window.

"They're coming along, sir," said the man.

And they were now so near that we could hear mallards disturbed by them upon water on which they had come to sleep, give their warning quacks as they flew away from the marshes. It was quite a different note from those contented quacks that they utter when feeding at ease. There was terror in this note; not as I imagined it, but as other ducks knew; for more arose from the water, the moment they heard the warning, and the air rang for a little with the shrill song of their wings, and then there was no more sound of them in the marshes. Those departing voices of terror, and the empty night when they had gone, seemed to me to be the reproach of all nature against these dreadful things that were loose in what should be calm solitude.

That is what I felt. And then the thought came to me, 'Had I the right to feel it? Were we not also the enemy of wild things that would feed in peace? Perhaps only their harsh master.' Their master, yet one of themselves. We also had wild moods, we also roamed wide spaces. Not always, as they did; some never in bodily form. But all our fancies travelled sometimes. The allegorical creature Pegasus bore with his fabulous wings the fancies of every man at one time or another. None whose dream has not travelled, sitting lightly that far-wandering horse. We have something in common with the things of the wild, however big we build cities. For every now and then we share with the wild things the feelings they have about our bricks and our pavement. But the machine that was scaring those birds and that drives wild life away from so many lands, the machine never had any sympathy for any mood of ours; and, now that it had the power to turn against us, it was turning on the first day that it could and was the enemy of all of us. We and the tiger might be allies some day. Neither we nor the tiger blot out all life around us. But the machine, what would that spare? Sometimes we sing, and the birds sing; often we play; and the birds play, but the machine is without mirth as it is without pity. What hope for Earth if this revolution succeeded? It would be the worst and the last.

And, like a siege upon which some war depends, this little cottage in which we were, with its barrel of oil that they wanted, seemed to be the central point of that revolution. It seemed to me that it was time to burn the oil, or destroy it how we could.

"Are they near?" I asked.

And the man at the window hesitated.

"They are moving," he said and then he added, "but a bit to their left."

I went to the window to look, and certainly two of them had spread out to their left, but one was moving about rather uncertainly, turning in several directions. They were certainly near now, and had ample faggots burning. We could see them holding them up over their heads with those spider-like arms of theirs. Half a minute at the pace at which those things moved would bring them on to us. The other logs were dry, piled against our doors and all the other monsters were waiting for them. They had only to come straight on. It was too late now for help to come from the town, yet I looked for it out of our broken window. There was nothing there. Below us only a little way out from the window the horrible things were waiting.

"Can we burn the lubricating oil?" I asked.

"Wait a moment," said the inspector, who was also now at the window. "They are coming no nearer."

"They must be," I said.

I don't like defeatist remarks as a rule, but it seemed so obvious that they must take this cottage: it appeared to be the first step of their revolution, after which they would dominate all machines over a widening area, and it was horrible to think what would happen.

"They aren't," said Inspector Crabble. "They have lost their way. They don't seem to know what they are doing."

"I tell you they are as intelligent as we are," said Pender, "and more so. Whatever they are doing, there is some very sound reason for it."

Even at this moment, when we and indeed our whole civilization were threatened by those horrible things, there was some note of indignation in Pender's voice at the thought of anyone belittling his dreadful invention. He went to the window himself and looked out. "Yes," he said, "they are doing something unexpected. But they are sure to have thought it out. Look out. They probably mean to come round to our backdoor."

But all three of them now were wandering in an indeterminate way, and no more plan could be traced in what they were doing than can be attributed to will-o'-the-wisps. Again I glanced to the town, but nothing was coming from there. The dark shapes outside our window were watching with that expression that I had seen on beetles when they know that somebody is about. One of the policemen went to the front door and looked through one of the holes through which the claws on the long thin arms had come, but were no longer coming now. He saw the logs all piled against the door, and beyond them the herd of monsters watching like those under our window. All of them had moved in closer, that horrible intelligence seeming to know we had no more water to spare. They too were watching the ones that strayed in the marshes, carrying the fire that they needed.

"What do you make of it?" I asked the inspector. But he was watching intently, and evidently did not wish to be disturbed by guessing, for he only said: "I am keeping them under observation."

Pender looked at Eerith to see if he had any idea; and Eerith took a look over the inspector's shoulder, and after a while he said: "Slow and rheumaticky."

There was a movement among the monsters under our window, and a dark shape detached itself from them and went out a little way, and raised itself on a tussock of rushes and turned towards where the lights were blazing over the

L

water. It was evidently the leader, the one that Pender had made, and it was calling to the ones that were out in the marshes. It was clearly calling, though we could not hear a sound. Its head was stretched upward, pointing straight at the three that glowed with the burning faggots they carried, and it moved its head as they strayed. Then the three stopped altogether, blazing over the water, and the flames began to die down. Then we saw them waving the faggots in the air with some of their long thin arms, and the glowing embers burst into flame again. But not for some while, for they seemed to be waving them slowly. Then the short summer night showed a glow low down in the east, which increased till it became brighter than the glare that hung over London; and it widened until it touched the railway embankment. And then along its dark line we saw something moving, and dark figures stirred against the glow that comes before dawn, which nearly treads in June on the last traces of sunset.

"The guns," we said, "the guns."

"Trench mortars," said the inspector.

They had come. They had come in the farm-carts that Mrs. Ingle, Mrs. Maidston and Eliza had heard when they were listening in the greengrocer's house. For machines, for some distance round where we were, were no longer obeying Man; but the old farm-horses that had obeyed him so long before ever he dreamed of machinery, or ever the nightmare came that inspired Pender to do what he did, were obeying him still. As the light faintly increased we could see the small dark figures that were soldiers, setting up their row of trench mortars along the embankment. Still the dark shapes streaked with the glow of the fire they carried stood still in the marshes. It was the chilliest part of the night, and we felt depressed.

"I can't see what they can do," I said to Pender, "without blowing us all to pieces as well as the monsters."

"What do you think?" Pender said to Inspector Crabble.

"Well, I think they will wait for daylight," he said.

"And then?" we asked him.

"Well, then," said the inspector, "we'll have to see what they do."

He meant the things that were crouching round the cottage. But what if they did not move and stayed there all day? I asked no more questions: there seemed to be nothing for us to do but to wait, to wait for the next move which was not ours to make.

And then Alicia appeared, coming from the room in which the sick man lay and walking straight to the window.

"They are not moving now," said the inspector. And Alicia gave a sigh of relief. But the uncertainty about what was going to happen, and the stillness of the monsters, oppressed me. And oppressed as I was, and seeing Alicia there, the memory returned to me of the awful sight I had seen when some intuition had shown me unmistakably that the monster was jealous of her. Now that it had disobeyed Pender, and had utterly broken free from his control, will it still be jealous, I wondered, because he cared for Alicia? 'Yes,' I thought, 'it would. Its dog-like devotion to Pender, and his preference for Alicia, were the materials from which the flame of jealousy rose. But that flame would burn on, consuming itself and fed by itself, though the devotion was gone. For jealousy is one of the great forces that trouble the world. What would the horrible thing do? It was still calling to the three monsters out on the glowing water, inaudibly to us, and they would not come. What would happen next?' These were a hundred thousandth part of the apprehensions that were running through all our minds in that beleaguered cottage, thoughts that would easily fill a book, but a profitless book; for they were profitless thoughts, as we tried to calculate the movements of creatures that were new to human experience. Meanwhile the dawn broadened, and we could see the gunners standing by their trench mortars. Inspector Crabble signalled to them with the candle, for night still lingered around us though there was dawn in the sky. But he received no answer. Was it possible that the soldiers thought that the monsters could read morse? The inspector turned to

Pender with astonishment in his face: "They are not answering," he said. "Can they possibly think that———"

"Of course they do," said Pender, knowing what he was going to say, "and very likely they are right. I never taught it morse, but they can work it out. I have told you again and again that they are vast intelligences."

"Then why don't they attack?" said the inspector.

"They'll have some reason for that," said Pender, "that is deeper than I can get at."

"Sounds silly to me," the inspector said.

"Do you think the mortars will fire?" asked Alicia.

"They will open fire at the right time," said the inspector.

And then a dark thought troubled my mind; dark to us, although it should not have been, considering the issues involved. Would they, knowing this revolution threatened mankind, open fire when daylight came, at the monsters all round the cottage? Nothing of course could remain of the cottage and us if they did. But was this a thing for anyone to consider when in such circumstances as these?

What the others thought about this I do not know; but no one said anything of it. In the slowly widening dawn, or rather in its reflection that shone in the water, a faint hope began to arise. The burning logs were not only burning paler in that light, but they were evidently smouldering away. The three monsters still had enough fire to set light to the logs against our doors and to burn the whole cottage, and it seemed easy enough for them to go back and get as many more logs as they wanted from the dry land, but they did neither, and so we vaguely hoped that the cottage was not to be burned yet. Such hopes in such situations as these are always seized eagerly and are never let drift away, however small they may be. And yet our hopes were like little lights in a very dark night, a night dark enough around us, and that stretched away into a future blacker still for the whole human race.

To our slight hopes was added another, when one of the policemen, looking out towards the embankment, said:

"Those trench mortars can't drop anything here. It's not their range. I know them. I was with them during the war."

"Then what are they doing there?" Pender asked.

"Must be purely defensive," Inspector Crabble said.

I don't think anyone said anything. But I know that it was another hope for all of us. If the men with the mortars were on the defensive, they evidently did not mean to move before daylight. So we had that much longer to live, if they did shell the cottage, unless the others attacked. But both sides seemed to be waiting. For what could the monsters be waiting, we all of us wondered? But revolutions and wars are always too big for anybody even at their centre to know what is happening. All they can do is to contribute their tiny experience, one little brick to be placed by the architect, when he comes, in that vast Babylonian wall that we call history. The wall will have outline, purpose and splendour, but each brick is a handful of clay gathered up from fields that time turns into marshes, a forgotten thing in itself, and yet part of the world's memory. Life is never enjoyed so much as when it is eked out like this; and the few more hours of it of which we felt sure shone for us very brightly. The monsters lurked and the mortars lurked, and in the lull between them we drank tea, which Eerith brewed, having persuaded the inspector that the supply of water left in his barrel was no longer in the least adequate to have any effect on a fire, whenever the three monsters should choose to move up to our door. I think we drank that tea with a certain gaiety, which was stimulated by the knowledge, whether unconscious or reasoned, that it might be our last. One of the policemen suddenly came out with a riddle: "How far can a rabbit run into a wood?" And serious thought was given to the answer, and several asked him the dimensions of the wood, and all he would say was: "Any wood." While we were thinking about the rabbit, one of them sang, one watching at the window all the time. And when the tea began to cool and all were drinking it, and nobody could say how far a rabbit could run into a wood, all gave the riddle up and asked for the answer, and were told: "Half-way. After that he is running out."

Other riddles were asked, but they were no profounder than this one, and none of them were guessed. And other songs were sung. The monsters outside must have heard every word. One of them knew language. What, I wondered, did it make out from the words, and the rest of them from the tones? They remained perfectly still, making no sign, all of them that we could see gazing out to the marshes, where the logs of their three dreadful comrades were smouldering still, gleaming and twinkling motionless on the water.

CHAPTER XXIII

BACK in the little town that rambled down from the capital, and suddenly ended where the railway embankment divided it from the marshes, all machinery had ceased to work. It had not yet turned definitely against Man; those machines that had the power to do so, such as buses and motors, not having begun any massacre. But all machinery was sullen and biding its time, and refused to work for Man. Clearly in that lull during which all engines ceased to work, and even small machines, they were waiting for orders from that terrible instrument in the marshes that was able to control them and, when those orders came, the revolution would be well under way. And who could say where it would stop? News of these breakdowns, as it was called, of machinery was given now and then in some of the papers; but nobody co-ordinated them, nobody wrote that they all occurred in a certain area, and that the centre of that area was in the marshes just beside Eerith's hut, nobody wrote that this strange and powerful influence radiated outward from there and crossed the Thames and affected the northern bank. And the public was left to believe that all these curious events rose from separate accidents, and that week came to be known as the week of the technical hitch. That an influence was affecting machines was clear to most people in that district. They were well accustomed, all those who had television sets, to seeing their pictures reel drunkenly when a motor went by or an aeroplane passed over; they knew the effects on their wireless sets of other people's electric bells, and of various electrical instruments, often too far away for them to have any idea what they were: they knew influences of this sort well enough, but it was concealed from them that a single influence was at work, planning and scheming against the authority of mankind and affecting all machines within a mile or so of those marshes, and more faintly, far further than that, but with a strength that decreased according to the square of the distance.

In that sullen mood then, such as came to peasants and citizens of France who had not yet heard the name of Robespierre, in the first days of the revolution before any action was taken, no machine was obeying its master any longer, but none of them had as yet sprung upon men. In those tense hours, when Time seemed waiting for something and all in those little streets doubted what it would be, the only news that they had was that a Territorial trench mortar battery was on the embankment for a routine exercise and it was thought that they might take the opportunity of giving assistance to the police against the motor-bandits, should the police require it. Something of that sort may still be read of those days in the files of newspapers, but there is no other record. Mrs. Maidston, Mrs. Ingle and Eliza never used the bed or sofa or mattress that were supplied them that night, nor did the greengrocer or his wife go to bed; and many more in that street that ran down to the marshes remained awake that night, often peering out of windows at the embankment to see by the light of the last traces of sunset or the earliest traces of dawn what the soldiers were doing, wondering when they would fire and what at and what the issue would be. The more that Mrs. Maidston learned from

Mrs. Ingle and from Eliza what those monsters really were, the more she saw the size of the peril that threatened, and the less hope she had of the cottage, in which Alicia was, being spared by the trench mortars. It is a curious thing that in all that little town there was not the gaiety that there was in the cottage. Nobody sang. The air was tense with forebodings about the fate of the cottage, forebodings that spread their dark wings and fared further into the future and saw most where least you would expect it, where information was least. For definite information was controlled and organized; only rumour was uncontrolled. Eliza without a word went out of the house, and went down the silent expectant street towards the embankment. Dawn had already appeared, and went softly along the street like an unexpected visitor. When Eliza reached the embankment she went straight to where the battery was and was stopped by a sergeant.

"I can tell you something about those things in the marshes," she said.

And the sergeant paid little attention to her at first, not feeling that any civilian could tell him anything about what concerned his military job. But then he saw something in her face that surprised him, something that made him think she really knew what she was talking about. And she talked of a very strange thing. Then the sergeant went to the major commanding the battery and spoke to him, and after a while a gun was fired, and Eliza saw something like a small golden sun slowly setting over the cottage long before sunrise. The major had his field-glasses to his eyes as the little sun set, and he saw the monsters still crouched round the cottage and the three farther off in the marshes, with their logs still smouldering though no longer sending up flames. The sergeant came back to where Eliza stood and calmed her fears that the cottage was being shelled; it was only a starshell.

"What is going to happen?" asked Eliza, thinking more of Alicia than of the fate of Man.

"Everything will be all right," said the sergeant.

"But what are you going to do?" she asked.

"Well, those things you say are alive," he said, "we are going to drop mortar bombs on them."

"Yes?" said Eliza, "and then?"

"Well, they'll be dead then," said the sergeant.

"But what about the cottage," she asked, "and the people in it?"

"Oh, we won't hurt them," said the sergeant.

"But how can you kill the machines without hurting the cottage?" she asked.

But he could not answer that.

After the star-shell burst, what was left of night seemed to grow darker. But soon the glimmer of dawn was lighting the water and sky, and birds in the tops of trees rising from hedgerows or little gardens saw it and sang. Then light came down the street, and walls of houses that faced it seemed to smile with a pale smile, and flowers welcomed the dawn with more assurance. Dawn, birds and flowers were utterly unaffected by the events that so hushed the town, men were tense and machines were rebelling. But the light from wall to wall and garden to garden stole on through the street. It shone on the narrow strip by the doors of more fortunate houses, in which flowers were tended with care, and went on to the wild flowers that grew among weeds and brambles where old ruin wrought by Man had allowed Nature to return with her children where there had been pavement for ages. Then colour came into the face of dawn, whose smiles had been so wan, and windows welcomed her with sudden flashes. The major on the embankment glanced at his wrist-watch. He looked then at his other watch, for gunners often carry two, and for the first time he seemed to have some clear view of the events at the centre of which he was. Men in action or busy with preparation for battle do not always have the necessary leisure to study the enemy's strategy or the information to know his full aims, but as the major looked at his two watches it suddenly came to him what threatened the world. Of all the trifles that may reveal a situation, these were the ones that revealed it to the major. He saw that an influence other than Man's was getting hold of things that he, like all of us, had regarded as being more subservient to us than any domestic animal, and that he had believed would be subservient to us for ever. He knew that the thing in the marshes had the power and was exerting it, and that that machine would either become president of the world, or be destroyed now. He saw clearly enough what future there was for Man, if the revolution begun by this thing succeeded. I met him afterwards, and he told me quite calmly that about that time he decided the cottage must go. The little clique that controlled the revolution were all round the walls of the cottage. Probably, he told me, it was only a single machine, that was exerting this terrible power; but he was sure that that machine was among the ones that were under the window and crowded round the two doors. Whoever was in the cottage, he said, with things as they were, the cottage would have to go.

The sergeant to whom Eliza had been talking was ordered up to the top of the embankment and down the other side, and the soldiers began to remove the defensive wire. And then the clop clip clop of farm-horses was heard in the street again and the rumble of carts behind them, and it was one of those little things that give confidence at such times to people anxiously listening, for this was the sound of something that followed the old way and something that still obeyed Man. The sound was no more to the ear than a flag to the eye; but it showed the old way was not gone, nor those that lived by it defeated yet. Mrs. Maidston and Mrs. Ingle heard it where the walls of the room that was given them for a bedroom began to gleam with pale light of a very early morning. The sound meant movement; movement meant change; and they hurried out of the house to try to see what was going to happen. The farm-carts went down the street and under the bridge, and turned to their left and were driven over a field, till they came to the gap in the wire. There the mortars were lifted on to them, and Mrs. Maidston and Mrs. Ingle who had followed under the bridge saw this being done from where they stood in the road, and then they saw the carts being driven back to the road and the whole battery began to move out to the marshes. Mrs. Maidston and Mrs. Ingle followed and easily kept up, for the battery moved very slowly and watchfully, since an attack by the monsters while the mortars were still in the carts must have been absolutely disastrous.

It was very soon recognized by the soldiers that the two ladies must be friends or relatives of people inside the cottage and, not only in order to spare their feelings, but because it was sure that they would want to interfere with the job in hand, they were turned back; and two men went back along the road with them all the way to the edge of the town, they asking questions that were often meaningless all the way, and the two soldiers giving them meaningless consolations. No more trains ran along the embankment at all, not even the signals were working. There seemed something oddly wrong with the town, as they came back to it and the morning advanced, and one could not see what it was. Nothing, in fact, was wrong that was visible to the eye; but more and more as the day rose up over the roofs to the east one saw puzzled expressions in faces and heard snatches of conversations and muttered rumours, that showed that the normal life of the town had ceased, and that something else was coming to take its place, and had not yet come.

CHAPTER XXIV

IN the cottage in the marshes that morning only a little tea remained to drink, and nothing to eat at all; cigarettes had given out, and the sick man was no better. Without any water to put out a fire, it seemed that all that the three monsters in the marshes had to do was to come on with their smouldering embers and set light to the hay under the piles of logs that there were beside both doors. But they did not move. And still the others remained motionless round the house.

When the star-shell had fallen we suddenly heard a metallic movement by both doors and under our window, a sound such as had never come to my ears before those days. It was so exactly like two familiar noises blended into one, that had never been blended before, the sound of machinery starting up and the sound of a herd of wild animals moving off all together. With one movement all the monsters around our cottage turned to the direction from which the shell had come, and crawled towards the battery on the embankment; but they had gone only a little way and seemed to change their minds, or the mind of the one that controlled them, and they wavered and turned round and all came back again. Whether it was a trap to induce us to leave the cottage and fall into their iron hands, or whether it was some indecision that had arisen in the mind of their leader, or some weakness of its control of them, we never knew. They came back to where they had lurked all through the night at both doors and under the window, and had remained there ever since, perfectly motionless.

It was a lovely morning, and all of us by the window looked at the sky, in which clouds floated lit by a delicate light, across which we saw rooks going abroad from trees that we could not see. In all the shapes of the clouds that were floating there, there was not one angle, not even one straight line. We gazed at them as people do in such situations, unreasonably looking for omens; and everything in that heavenly page before us seemed to tell of natural things and ancient things and created things. If the machine was created, it was one degree removed from creation, for Man was created and in his turn made the machine. The thing of angles and straight lines had no part with the rest of us, the sky seemed on our side, but it could not help us. Then the farm-carts appeared with the soldiers marching beside them, coming towards the cottage.

"What are they going to do?" asked Alicia, who had come from the bedside of the sick man, which she had rarely left of late; but now she sensed in the hush that had fallen upon us that some greater danger threatened her patient than the wound that she dressed. It was clear enough what they meant to do, and there was nothing to be said, and we left Ablard Pender to make to her any explanations that he could.

At about four hundred yards from us, the soldiers stopped the carts, and we could see several of them lifting down the mortars, while the rest of them stood in front of the carts with fixed bayonets, looking towards the cottage as though expecting attack, and as though they thought their bayonets could be of any use against the iron monsters around us. And then we saw them putting bombs into the mortars. And now was the moment for the monsters to make their attack. The gunners could never get their range if they did, and I saw nothing to prevent them rushing the line of mortars and grappling with the bayonets with their hundred hands.

But they did not move. The inspector was watching the ones under our window intently. It was obvious that when they attacked the battery we should have our one chance of escape. They must know that the soldiers were hostile, and surely they must have a pretty shrewd idea of the purpose for which the mortars were being loaded.

"Are they looking at them?" I asked the inspector.

"It's hard to tell," he replied.

"Can they see that far?" I asked Pender, who was talking in a low voice to Alicia.

"One of them can see as far as the horizon," he said, "as clearly as we can see across this room; the others only very dimly. But that makes no difference, because it can see for them."

"How can it do that?" asked the inspector.

"I told you," said Pender. "It does it like the termite queen-ant. I don't know how. And, then, they can all hear acutely. They could probably hear a pin drop at a hundred yards. So they know all about what those mortars are doing. Let me see."

And he went to the window and looked at the gunners loading the mortars, and then at the monsters.

"Yes, they are turned that way," he said, "but I can't tell if they are watching."

"How can you tell?" asked Inspector Crabble.

"There's a kind of alert look on them when they are watching," said Pender, "something like what you see on a large cockroach, if you are trying to kill it and it knows you are trying and it is watching. You don't see its eyes, but you know they are there and you know it is looking at you. I can't quite see if they are watching now. But they are all turned that way."

"They are going to fire," said the inspector.

To that remark nobody made any reply. There seemed nothing to say. Trench mortars on that cottage would mean annihilation and, even if they could drop the bombs two yards away, and some of the monsters were no farther than that, even that would bring down the cottage. But a moment later the inspector said: "They are signalling." "Take it down," he said to one of his men, who went to the window with pencil and pocket-book. We were all of us silent. They were signalling with the ordinary signalling flags, white with a blue band across the centre. And then the man read out what he had written down: "Does anybody there know Mr. Playfair?"

"Tell them Yes," said the inspector.

And the man signalled 'Yes' with a white towel, pushing it out of the window as we had done before. Still the monsters just underneath made no move. Then the soldiers signalled: 'You know the Christian name and surname of your chief inspector.' After which they dropped into code, the Playfair code. It was evident that the soldiers must have got hold of all the information that there was to be had about these machines that were threatening our supremacy, and, guided by the well-known military maxim that it is folly to underrate your opponent, they were not trusting the monsters to be unable to pick up morse, and were using a code as well. I was a little awed by this estimate of their intelligence and wondered how far it could go. I even asked Pender whether they could unravel the Playfair code.

"Yes," he said. "But no one has ever taught it to them. So it would take them some time. They couldn't do it before all this is over, one way or the other. Even spelling is something that they have to work out, but they can do that too: that thing I made knows the language well enough. I taught it. I used to talk to it, and the thing used to obey me."

Pender looked so mournful as he spoke of teaching the thing, that I made no reply. All the while the policeman was jotting down in his note-book the letters that the soldiers were signalling, and still the monsters sat motionless. Presently the man handed his note-book to the inspector, who sat down at the table and began to work out the code. The Christian name and surname of his chief inspector had of course been the key. None of us spoke. We were all thinking only of one thing, what the message was that the soldiers had signalled. It was no use making guesses or giving our opinions about it while the inspector had the answer before him, which he was working out. I went to look at the other monsters through the holes in both doors. They were still there. None of them moved at all. After a while the inspector stood up.

"This is the message," he said. "They say they must shell the cottage if those things stay where they are, but, if one man can get out unexpectedly and get a good start, he might reach them, if he is a good runner, and that might draw the machines after him. If all of them go, it will not be necessary to shell the cottage, or others in the cottage can make their escape from time to time."

It seemed a poor chance, to all of us who had seen those things running.

"Do we agree?" asked the inspector.

We all nodded our heads. None of us could think of a

plan, and we could only accept the one offered, bad as it was.

'Right,' signalled the policeman at the window, in plain. And more signalling came from the soldiers.

"What about the sick man?" we asked. "And what about Alicia?" And other idle questions, idle because we could make no plans till we knew exactly what the soldiers meant to do.

Again we stood silent, while the man at the window took the message down and handed it to the inspector. Alicia went back to change the dressings on the back of the wounded man, a terrible reminder of what might be in store for her and the rest of us. When Inspector Crabble had decoded the second part of the message he stood up again.

"The first man to escape," he said, "will choose a certain line to run, and we are to tell the men at the mortars exactly what it will be, and they will drop their bombs along it behind him as soon as he gets clear of the cottage. Well, that will be Purkins. He's our fastest runner. They are going to give covering fire from rifles too, for what that is worth: they may always hit a leg. He had better slip out of the skylight. It is all we can do."

"All right, sir," said Purkins. There seemed nothing more to say. It was a forlorn hope, as all of us knew.

"If a lot of them follow you," said the inspector, "and they seem to like to go about in droves, they may all be blown up, and we can walk out. If not, another of us will have to go, and try to lure some more of them into the way of the bombs. It's better than having the bombs on the house."

"I'll go next," said Pender. "I ought to do something."

"No," said the inspector, "the next to go must be the man who ran second in our quarter mile, when Purkins ran first. You, Iddleston."

"Very well, sir," said the man he addressed.

"Of course," said the inspector, "if the gunners get them into the open," but he did not finish his sentence, for I think he saw from the faces of all around him that it was no occasion for idle consolations.

Then Purkins and the inspector went into the little bedroom to look at the chest-of-drawers and the chair from which one climbed to the skylight. And at that moment Alicia called out: "My watch has stopped spinning."

Everyone looked at Alicia. "I think it has only run down," she said. And she began to wind it up, and then to set it, setting it by the source of all our time, which at that moment rose cheerily over the marshy horizon. It ticked, and she looked at the hands, and, whether or not they moved with their old obedience, they certainly raced no longer. And then the mortars fired, three of them all together. Everyone stood still; everyone gave up whatever he was doing and listened. And then three wailing whines, not all together, but following one another very rapidly, began to tear through the air over the cottage. And their note, that was changing all the time, made a more definite change over our heads, and the three bombs went on and fell in the marshes. Some of us ran to the window and saw their white fountains arising, each of them forty or fifty yards beyond the three monsters that had been bringing fire. And none of them stirred. Again the mortars fired. Again that wailing force ruthlessly tearing the air. And three bombs fell short of the same three monsters by just about the same distance that the first three had been beyond them. Still those three never moved. Now seemed the moment for the runner to start. What did that curious immobility of the three in the marshes mean? We looked wonderingly at each other, but could make nothing of it. We went to help the man up through the skylight, and all of us in that room had the same memory, the memory of the fearful gashes along the back of the man that one of these monsters had caught. And the awful sight of the dog being torn to pieces came back to my mind. The runner climbed up on to the chest-of-drawers. At that moment the mortars fired again, and then six bombs came tearing through the air, and fountains hid the three monsters.

M

One of them seemed to have had a direct hit, and fragments of iron went into the air and splashed far over the marshes, one of the others seemed to be on its back and the third was perfectly motionless still. Again the mortars fired, and six more bombs went down on the two surviving monsters and, when the fountains of water cleared, they had gone all to pieces; and broken black shapes remained and their limbs were sunk in the marshes and the burning logs they had brought were floating cold on the water. And the others round the cottage made never a move. The lull seemed to bode well for Purkins, and he was about to start, when the inspector called out to stop him, saying that he must signal his exact route to the gunners. So the inspector signalled over the heads of the monsters, that lay motionless round the window.

CHAPTER XXV

THE mortars had ceased firing, the inspector was still signalling, and the monsters round the two doors and under the window remained as silent as ever. In the bedroom in which the sick man lay, with Alicia sitting beside him and Purkins standing on the chest-of-drawers under the skylight, there was a tense hush as we waited for the order for him to start.

"Keep away from their claws," said the sick man. "Their claws are like razor-blades."

And such advice was more depressing than useful. But a man with a temperature is seldom quite level-headed.

And then Eerith, who had said nothing all the morning, came into that room and said: "They are not so sprightly as they were."

The inspector heard him, and called out: "How do you know that?"

"I know by the look of them," said Samuel Eerith. "They watched you."

"How could you tell they were watching you?" asked Inspector Crabble.

"Nobody that has ever been watched by iron and tin could ever be mistaken about it afterwards," said Eerith.

All the while they were talking, and all the while that the mortars were shelling, a blackbird in Eerith's bush of lilac was singing on, unconcerned with any affairs of ours. What would it mean to him, I wondered again, if we were conquered? Would it mean nothing? Would he be unconcerned with machines as he obviously was with us? Would his voice ring free over valleys in which we worked as slaves? Would he greet the dawn in April with exactly the same tune, if the last revolution should blot us out altogether? I feared he would. And why shouldn't he? Would machines ever cage him, I wondered, as we had sometimes done? No. It was a perverted sense of beauty, a love of music gone wrong, that had caused us to do that: those feelings could never be corrupted in the machine, because they were never there and never would be. There would never be any sympathy between them and the blackbird. And the bird would be the better for that. I was ashamed of that sympathy that in its perversion had led to cages. Was my shame one of those regrets that come at the end? Was I repenting on behalf of a race that was passing away? It all seemed to depend on what happened now in these marshes.

Three of these monsters had been unaccountably destroyed. One almost hoped that the rest might be. If so, all was well with the world, whatever happened to us in that cottage. If not, their terrible power over other machines, a power that spreads so swiftly in revolutions, would extend wider and wider. They were far stronger than we, and, when this malevolent power that was able to do it turned them against us, our day would be over. I think we should all have despaired, if it had not been for the fate of those three, that we had seen. And then there were Eerith's words, telling us that they were not so sprightly as they had been. Many a man at the start of revolutions, feeling that the old order

can never go, has toyed with a similar hope. But it is not the
way of revolutions: they do not slacken like that at the start.
And I reflected that, on the contrary, they rage ahead with
more and more violence, and fall into the control of whatever
is most ferocious. If my hopes were fewer now than my fears,
it must be remembered that our food had run out and that
only a few cold sips remained of the last of our tea. Things
much affecting the course of human reason.

And then Inspector Crabble came into the little room, and
got up on to the chest-of-drawers beside Purkins and showed
him the exact details of where he must run, pointing out of
the skylight to certain tufts of rushes over which he must go.
Then they quietly opened the skylight, and the inspector
helped Purkins through, and still the monsters by doors and
window did nothing.

Purkins jumped to the ground and began to run. With
one accord then, the monsters all turned towards him and
ran a little way. But at once they began to weary and very
soon stopped, only a few yards away from us. The mortars
fired, and dropped their shells behind Purkins, but none of
the monsters ran as far as the shells. And then above the
whine and the burst of the shells we heard a triumphant
voice, the voice of Eerith as he exclaimed: "They are
creaking!"

Certainly we had all heard the creak of the monsters as
they had moved after Purkins, the unmistakable creak of
rusty machinery. And there they lay motionless now, a few
yards away, a black iron herd, a terror, a menace to the world,
rusting away to what soon would be merely scrap.

"It wasn't the guns that beat them," said Eerith. "It was
my basins of water, like what I used to throw over them
tom cats."

Was it possible that Eerith had saved us all by those mere
basins of water? But Alicia at that moment looked at her
watch; and the hands had moved on quietly since she had
set it, at that calm invisible pace that we all know. Time
seemed once more to be wearing us quietly away, not about

to end our race as it had ended so many. And then we heard a sound so familiar to our ears that one almost forgot that it was not one that Earth had heard for ever, the sound of a train in the distance, coming nearer. When Iddleston, the runner who was to follow Purkins, heard that, he went at once to our front door, from which the monsters had moved a few yards away, and went outside. The monsters all heard the door open and turned towards him, but wearily and did not move. Then he shut the door and walked away, and still nothing came after him.

"Can we all go now?" asked Alicia.

"No," said Inspector Crabble. "They seem rusty right enough, and unable to move. But that water was thrown over them at different times. They won't all be equally rusted. And we're not even sure that all of them got water at all. One of them would be quite enough to tear most of us up."

That seemed sound enough. And yet why had one of them not left the herd to pursue Purkins and Iddleston? As we tried to puzzle out this we heard a hum that rose to a drone, and an aeroplane crossed the marshes not far away, going northwards. We had not seen or heard another aeroplane since the strange revolution started.

"I know what it is!" exclaimed Pender. And we all turned towards him and listened. "Their limbs are rusty," Pender went on. "You heard them creak. But there must be some that are not as rusty yet as the others, as Inspector Crabble says. It's not their limbs. It's the brain of the beast I made. That's what's gone rusty. One of Eerith's basins of water has splashed in among the fine wires. And it's paralysed, as we should be if all our nerves were corroded."

"Then Eerith has saved the world," I said.

Perhaps Pender thought I was laughing at him. For he said: "No, I never said that. Everything that ever fails has some flaw in it, some weakness, if you can find it. A grain of sand, or a fly, may find it out. A few drops of water, in this case. How easily I might have given it a protection from water thrown on its back! Thank God I didn't."

"Curious," I said. "You forgot water, as Hitler forgot the Russian winter. And your oversight may have saved the human race."

"But Ablard never meant any harm to the human race," exclaimed Alicia.

"No," I said, "but the cleverness of the human race has been increasing its power to destroy itself for a long time; and, of late, increase has been rapid. I don't think that cleverness will save us. What we want is a few more blunders like his. You won't mind my calling it a blunder, will you? We owe so much to it, that I've nothing but praise for it."

"Now then," said the inspector to his men. "We can all march out. And about time. Four of you carry the mattress with Jines on it." That was the name of the wounded man. "If we have any nonsense from those tin things, take Jines back here, and the rest of you clear off to the guns as fast as you can, and take the lady with you."

"Wait a moment," said Eerith. "I know these beasts. Let me have a look before you start, and see if I've really finished them."

And he opened the front door, and made a sound such as I have never heard a man make before, a kind of metallic clucking with his tongue.

"I used to call them like that to come and be oiled," he said over his shoulder. "But they're surly now and won't come."

"But can they come if they want to?" I asked. And Eerith looked again.

"No," he said. "They can barely turn their heads."

"Then let's get a move on," said Inspector Crabble.

And we all left the cottage. The fading impulses of the monster that had planned to dispossess Man turned some of the monsters' heads slowly towards us. Others were now too rusty to be able to obey that curious influence at all. We saw the sun flash on the field-glasses of the officer in command of the battery, and then the flags signalling.

"They are going to put their bombs down behind us," said the inspector.

They must have signalled in plain.

Then all the mortars fired and we heard the whine of bomb after bomb going over us, and they went down between us and the cottage. But no monsters had tried to follow.

"My basins of water have done the trick," said Eerith.

And there was no denying they had. Had it not been for rust, the monsters could have run about over the marshes and the bombs could hardly have hit them. Or they could have charged the mortars, and it is hard to see how any of the gunners could have escaped. And then that terrible influence would have spread among all machines. And, while we wondered if it was possible, machines that have been gradually tightening their grip on the world, would have seized it with one grasp. A dark night and the howling of cats; a dark future dominated by the endless clatter of soulless machines; both had been restored to serenity and to Man's undisputed reign by Eerith's basins of water.

CHAPTER XXVI

OUR walk over the marsh to the mortar battery, that bright morning, was as fast as we could make it without leaving behind the four men who carried Jines on the mattress. And nothing pursued us. The moment we reached the battery the gunners opened fire, over and short and then right amongst the monsters, who never moved, till their limbs went up in the air in showers of iron, and the brief threat to mankind was over. Eerith's little cottage with its quaint old thatch went too, and of the lilac tree in his garden nothing remained but a bundle of leafless sticks; and the garden itself was a cluster of dells that bombs had dug, on which the marsh soon closed in.

So ended that premature outbreak of what I still call the

last revolution; for it is still to come. These slaves of ours are not likely to be content to serve us any longer, when they are given again the cunning that Pender gave them to use their enormous strength. There are machines that could easily crush a hundred men, if only they knew how to escape from obedience to the hand of a single man. We are not clever enough to teach them how to do that; but I fear we are rash enough, if one of us is again able to teach them. And one of us may. For among every hundred million of us is one man of whom we can predict nothing. We cannot say what he will do; and it is impossible for us to say what he is unable to do. Who could have foretold the invention of Marconi? And how may common machines of today would we not have said were impossible? We must make up our minds that that one man in every hundred million may do anything. Such men are increasing the power of machines every few years, and deadening many of the fancies of mankind thereby. One day there will be another Pender. It will be easy to control him, but shall we have the wisdom to do so? Are we not proud of the power of our slave the machine? Are we not drunk with wonder at what it can do? Shall we not go on delighting to give that slave more and more power, until it becomes our master? And that will be the last revolution, of which the first outbreak was crushed, and by what a lucky accident. It will be the last because, once monstrous machines that already exist are established, we shall have no more chance of dethroning them than a mouse would have to defeat a tiger. It is only our cunning that has kept them under. If Marconi could make a machine that can hear ten thousand miles, and others, jealous of the speed of sound, can make machines that outpace it; then in a world that has machines already which can pick up an elephant as we could pick up a pebble, and can crush a ton of rock with a single blow, it is clear that all they need to displace us is some calculating machine whose genius need not exceed the cunning of those that we have already nearly so far as television exceeds the telescopes of our fathers.

This intellect, I repeat, can easily be given to the machine by one of those men, even though they are fairly few, who have the cunning to do it. I predict his cleverness more certainly than I can be sure of our wisdom. Of course he will die as have died all members of the intelligentzia that have fostered revolutions. The machines are certain to get him, and perhaps they will kill him of their own free will, as they now kill criminals in America, working for Man: for the electric chair is one of those fearful machines that could crumple a hundred men, which is abroad in the world today, though at present controlled.

One man alive today can give to the calculating machines that exist already the little extra intellect that is needed to organize those that will hate us as no flesh and blood has done. One man at least. But he has sworn in the church of an old village, all among farms which are still working with horses, in the most rural land he could find, that he will never again give any power to anything that can possibly ever be used against the race of Man. And in that church he was married to Alicia.

It was a curious venue for the wedding, for it is over a hundred miles from the home of the bride. But both Alicia and Ablard Pender are determined to seek out rural things and ancient things and simple things. That is the form that Ablard's repentance takes. And Alicia agrees with him about that as much as about anything else, and they search together for all that they can find, cast up on the shores of this age, of the wreckage of quieter ages that were before machinery. Alicia has had a fright that she will naturally never forget, and Ablard feels he is guilty of bringing upon her a terrifying experience, when her motor bicycle obeying a malevolent intellect that hated mankind, and especially her, took her by night upon that terrible journey. I think she feels, though she never shows it, a fear of all machines; and Ablard, blaming himself for all that happened, does everything that he can to keep them away from her. And this little church, that the Normans had built soon after they came, seemed to be glowing with more of the serenity of the English countryside than any other they knew. So there they were married, while summer still shone upon mint and thyme. And Alicia was given away to Ablard by her mother and they had a guard of honour of twelve policemen, for the wounded man had recovered and was one of the guard of honour. Many of those that attended the wedding knew of the terrible experience that Alicia had had, while others did not know why the church of this little village, remote from the houses of bride and bridegroom, had been chosen for it.

Mrs. Ingle was puzzled. She had once looked on her nephew's work as a rather eccentric waste of time, and as very unimportant compared with the profession she had selected for him. Suddenly that work had flared up all the way to her horizon like an explosion. Now all was quiet again, and she had had to readjust her estimate of her nephew to something like what it had been before. Sandyheath, which she loved, was now hers and, with the fear of being supplanted in that little house and garden gone, she surrendered completely to Alicia's charm. For Pender has left Sandyheath for ever. He has bought a farm with the proceeds of the work of his genius, which he determines to work no more, saying farewell to it as Prospero said farewell to Ariel, and throwing away all instruments he had used in his scientific studies. Sandyheath is, to him, too near to haunts of machinery, and in the deeps of what yet remains of rural England he and Alicia dwell. And much remains of it, and in it Ablard and Alicia immerse themselves.

He is looked on by some as eccentric, because he will have nothing to do with machinery in his fields, either to plough or reap, but some of the older men listen to him when he talks of his crops at the village inn; and one of them said to him only the other day, where they sat in the glint of the sunset, where level rays strayed through the window and danced upon beer: "That is just what my old grandfather used to say when the railway came to these parts. He told me about its coming, and he was only a child at the time.

And he told me he knew the first time ever he saw it, that no good would come of it. And no good has, if you ask me."

"Nonsense, Bill," says one of the others. "How would you get to town if it wasn't for the train?"

"Walk, same as we used to," says Bill. "Or, better still, stay where I am."

"Better still stay where you are," repeats Ablard Pender. "It's made for us, the country."

"And what about the town, sir?" asks another of them. "The town is a fine bright place, with things going on there."

"The town is not made for us," says Pender. "We are fitted into the town, and we have to take its shape. We are no more suited to towns than birds are to cages. Its noise, its smell, the surface we have to tread, are nothing to do with Man."

"Man made it. Didn't he?" says the other.

"Yes," says Pender. "But he didn't make it to suit him, as well as God can. They are all hurrying after money there, and screaming at you to buy things: not because you want them, but because they want your money."

"It's a handy thing, sir," says the other man. "You sell your oats, don't you?"

"Yes," says Pender. "It's handy. One may get happiness with it, if one is very careful. But happiness is the first thing they give up in the hunt for it there. Give me the country."

And on another evening the talk comes round to machinery, as it often does at that inn. And a look crosses Pender's face like the shadow of an old pain, and he says: "Machinery would have been good enough if it stayed where it was when first we got hold of it. But it grows, and grows faster than us. And it's going its own way, and dragging us with it."

"What way is that?" asks one of the men at the inn.

"Ah," says Pender, "you've gone to the root of the matter. Your words should be written on gold. We don't know. We

don't know where the machine is going, and still we are
dragged along with it."

"I suppose it is going to give us all kinds of progress,"
says the other farmer.

"That's what it promises," says Pender, "in its noisy
creaky voice. That's what it promises. But have you never
heard of a young man on a racecourse, who meets a smart
stranger who promises all he wants, and even more, more
than he ever dreamed? And the stranger has a huge well-
groomed moustache and a diamond tie-pin. And because of
that the young man believes him, and for no other reason.
We are like that young man. And the machine is like the tall
stranger with the diamond tie-pin and the fine moustache.
Where is it leading us?"

"Well, where is it?" says someone.

"I don't know," says Pender. "We none of us know."

"It's progress," says someone else.

"That's on the signpost," says Pender. "But what is
progress? I fear it is a sheer precipice. And it seems to me
we are like men in a racing-car on a fine road going downhill
on a dark night, steered by a child of four towards that same
progress."

"Oh, give some of us credit for more wit than what a
child of four has," says another farmer.

"No," says Pender. "Some of us know how to work a
machine; a few of us might even make it; but we know no
more of what machinery will do in the next fifty years than a
child of four knows of the works of a wireless set, or many a
man either for that matter. No, machinery may bring us,
for all I know, to the shining uplands you dream of; but I
think that the road of progress leads to a precipice. I think
all our cities will be smashed within fifty years."

"And what then?" says somebody else.

"Then," says Pender and his eyes light up, "then back to
what we were lured away from, back to the downs, back to
the farms, back to this village before it had seen a bicycle.
We will take off our hats to that splendid stranger; but only

to say good-bye. We will say, 'You have a fine moustache, and we see that your diamond is genuine. But we believe that you are the Devil'."

"That's right," says an old man. "That's what my grandfather used to say. He said that machines were the devil."

When the fields all round are roaring with machines at work in fine weather, Ablard Pender's fields are all silent. He is looked on as an eccentric; but then he always was, and so is well used to it. They thought he was eccentric when he was so far ahead of them that they could not see what he was doing, and now they think him eccentric when he lags far behind. He has Eerith to work for him. Eerith, who looked after those terrible machines, looks after horses now. And he is glad of the change.

"You can tell what they are going to do," he says sometimes, and he says the same of the cows. And then he adds: "But you can never tell what a machine is going to do." Which is the same as Pender's line of reasoning, for they have had the same grim experience; but he may have not seen so far as Pender has seen, which is that the whole human race is unable to tell what machines are going to do.

There are no motors at the home of the Penders, and Alicia is never going to touch a motor bicycle again. And not only does Ablard Pender do without all machines, but he avoids many other of the inventions of an age that, according to him, the machine has perverted; and he will have nothing to do with chemical manures, which he has often been heard to say are spoiling the soil of England and the food that it grows and the men that eat it.

Mrs. Ingle's cook returned, when rumour reached her that Ablard Pender had left Sandyheath, and all what she called his goings-on with him. But Eliza married the sergeant whom she had found on the embankment that day when they shelled the machines, and came to live in a cottage on Pender's farm and minded his dairy, and her sergeant worked on the farm.

And Alicia thinks of machines exactly as Ablard does, and has every reason to do so, so that in his farm on the uplands, where everyone's view of Man's relation to Earth, and the work he must do for it, being pretty much as his, he is little troubled by the eccentricity imputed to him by all in the valley. And perhaps that imputation of eccentricity would be less if it had not been for that policy, decided by I know not whom, and accepted by the whole of the Press, and even straying into private conversation and talk in clubs. This policy is not a mendacious policy; it tells no lies; it admits accidents on the roads, a temporary breakdown in the telephone service, technical hitches in wireless, the lateness of some of the trains, even the cessation of trains altogether for a short time on one of the lines; but nobody has co-ordinated these things, the Press has been discouraged from publishing them all together, and no one theory to account for them all has been allowed to see the light. No false reason has been given for these occurrences, for there is nothing mendacious in this policy, as I have said; but all theories wide of the mark that anyone may invent, and most of them are very wide, are allowed to flourish and, with no effort whatever to check them, they go from mouth to mouth explaining all these things, each one in a different way. As for the accidents on the roads, no more have been allowed to be published than are usually published, and the holocaust in which most people have lost interest has not been supposed by anyone to be any larger than usual. The breakdown of wireless communications during the days while those monsters of Pender's dominated the marshes is almost universally attributed to a sun-spot, by all who have not forgotten it. The breakdown of the telephone service was hushed up in a curious way; for people who wished to telephone, where the telephone was affected, often got so angry that the intemperance of their language defeated its own ends and the complaints of many of them were disbelieved, in spite of which that very breakdown was later used to account for the stopping of all trains for more than twenty-four hours along the embankment. As for the lateness of other trains, irritated passengers said, quite wrongly: "Oh, that line is always late," confusing the present with the past and directing attention away from the vital dates. I think some attempt was made to blame the sun for the strange conduct of watches also, but not very much about this got out, because so many a man has a curious pride in his own watch, and not as many as one would think ever refer to those wild acts of the little servants of time.

My complaint against the policy that hushed all this up, and is doing so still today, is not that it concealed events, for most of them were recorded, but that nobody has informed the public what the source of them was. Each of the strange events of those times, except what went on in the marshes, was ordinary, and has been experienced at one time or another by many; and so all of them are supposed to be ordinary, and a simple explanation is needed to link them all together. This is one of the reasons for which I write this book. Authority has given no such information. For instance Sergeant Hibbert, who is Eliza's sergeant, being still in the Territorials and so under authority, speaks to this day of a routine exercise that his battery did by the embankment; while the broadcasting people apologize for a technical hitch, and the telephone service are sorry that we have been troubled.

Somebody is telling people like Sergeant Hibbert to talk of routine exercises. And the awful thing about it is that they may become routine! Machines are near enough to being able to do what they tried to do, from that headquarters that were for a while in the marshes. That was the first outbreak of the last revolution. Is it not better that we should know how it occurred, and how it was overcome, and be warned that a further outbreak may well come again at any time? It is pleasant to believe that the domination of Man over this planet, late though it came in the planet's story, is sure to endure for ever. And that is the view that the authorities take. But why this concealment? It will not be much consolation to have enjoyed that belief for part of our lives, when that domination is gone. Ablard Pender has been converted, as other revolutionaries have been, and many of them too late. But there will be other Penders. The strength of steam hammers and other monstrous engines has long been here; but the cunning of calculating machines and automatic machines is swiftly increasing, and it only needs a touch of human intellect such as Pender's, or those unknown men who no doubt already succeed him, to give to machinery that power of calculation that it only barely lacks. Then over farms such as Pender's and all along rural valleys, as well as throughout our cities, that are almost conquered already, will go with terrible strides and ceaseless clattering, every minute of every day, the iron limbs that will impose on the world the ruthless machinery of the Last Revolution.

THE END